The Capricorn Bracelet

Also available in

Red Fox Classics

The Wolves of Willoughby Chase by Joan Aiken

Charlotte Sometimes by Penelope Farmer

Emil and the Detectives by Erich Kästner

Emil and the Three Twins by Erich Kästner

The Story of Doctor Dolittle by Hugh Lofting

The House of Arden by E. Nesbit

Swallows and Amazons by Arthur Ransome

Beowulf by Rosemary Sutcliff

The Hound of Ulster by Rosemary Sutcliff

The High Deeds of Finn MacCool by Rosemary Sutcliff

Sword Song by Rosemary Sutcliff

The Mennyms by Sylvia Waugh

Red Fox Classics

The Capricorn Bracelet

Rosemary Sutcliff

Illustrated by Charles Keeping

RED FOX

THE CAPRICORN BRACELET
A RED FOX BOOK 0 09 943217 X

First published in Great Britain in 1973 by Oxford University Press

First Red Fox edition published 1990
This Red Fox edition published 2002

1 3 5 7 9 10 8 6 4 2

Red Fox Books are published by Random House Children's Books,
61–63 Uxbridge Road, London W5 5SA,
a division of The Random House Group Ltd,
in Australia by Random House Australia (Pty) Ltd,
20 Alfred Street, Milsons Point, Sydney, NSW 2061, Australia,
in New Zealand by Random House New Zealand Ltd,
18 Poland Road, Glenfield, Auckland 10, New Zealand,
and in South Africa by Random House (Pty) Ltd,
Endulini, 5A Jubilee Road, Parktown 2193, South Africa

THE RANDOM HOUSE GROUP Limited Reg. No. 954009

www.kidsatrandomhouse.co.uk

A CIP catalogue record for this book is available from the British Library.

Printed and bound in Great Britain by
Bookmarque Ltd, Croydon, Surrey

Author's Note

The stories in this book began as scripts about Roman Scotland, which I wrote for Radio Scotland to produce as part of a series called 'Stories from Scottish History'. I loved writing them, but I got very cramped and frustrated by all the things I wanted to put in but had to leave out because there wasn't room for them in a twenty-minute script. So I decided, when the B.B.C. had finished with them, to write them again, as a book, in which I could have all the space I wanted for what I had to leave out before.

You will not find much about battles or big-scale historical events in *The Capricorn Bracelet* – something, but not much, because it is not meant to be that kind of book (and you can read about the battles and big-scale historical events elsewhere, anyway). It is just a collection of stories about people and changing ways of life over three hundred years or so, seen for the most part through the eyes of six members of a soldier family serving on or north of Hadrian's Wall. But for those of you who want to put the stories in their historical setting, and see exactly where they fit, and what happened between them, I have put an historical outline at the end of each chapter.

All the forts and towns mentioned in the book are real, but in a few cases, their Roman names are lost, and in those cases I have used the modern ones which replaced them. You may think it would be more consistent to use the modern names all through; but none exist for some of the forts and stations which are today a few grey stones half lost in cotton-grass and heather . . .

Placenames

AQUAE SULIS	Bath
CAMULODUNUM	Colchester
CILURNUM	
CORSTOPITUM	Corbridge
CREDIGONE	
EBURACUM	York
ISCA SILURUM	Caerleon-upon-Usk
LONDINIUM	London
LUGUVALLIUM	Carlisle
ONNUM	
SEGEDUNUM	Wallsend
TRIMONTIUM	Newstead
VERULAMIUM	St Albans
BODOTRIA AEST	The Forth
TAVA FL.	The Tay

Contents

I
Death of a City AD 61

They tell me that Londinium is rebuilt, fine and grand so that anyone who knew it in the old days would hardly know it again. But I shan't go back to see. Isca Silurum is my city now, headquarters of the Second Augustan Legion. And anyway, looking back, it seems to me that Londinium in the old days was as fine as any city needs to be – oh, not as I saw it last, fire-blackened and stinking of death, but in the time before the Killer Queen came down on us: the time when I was a boy.

It was a rich and busy merchant town already, with shipping coming and going up and down the broad river or lying alongside the crowded wharves and jetties. There was a great Forum where the markets were held and the people gathered on all kinds of public occasions; a basilica ran along one side of it, where the Magistrates met to govern the city. There were temples and bath houses and long straight streets where the noise of carts and hooves and chariots and feet went on all day and most of the night. It was a very new city, mind you; in fact, in places, it was still something of a shanty town, because we – the Romans, that is – had been less than twenty years in Britain.

Our house was in the street of the Amber Dolphin, not far from the river. Just a small house, with a bay laurel bush for Apollo growing in the courtyard, and my father's warehouse and cellars next door with their own gateway to the street. My father was a wine merchant, and as soon as I grew old enough to handle the mule, I was often given the task of taking wine up to the fort that guarded the town. He wanted me to have learned the family business from the bottom up, when the time came for me to take it over from him. It was a good idea – it's always a good idea to know one's business from the bottom up – but it didn't work out quite as he expected, because those visits to the fort made me want to be a soldier and not a wine merchant at all.

I kept my desire to myself for quite a while, for I knew what my father would think of it. And then, one evening when I was setting out the draughts board – my father liked me to play draughts with him sometimes after supper, when he was not too busy with his accounts – I simply came out with it, not even knowing that I was going to, until the thing was said and past unsaying again.

Why that evening, and not any other, I'll never know. My father had been talking a lot about the business over supper, but then he often did; and I don't think I had even been up to the fort that day. But I suppose I was thinking about it and not attending properly to what I was doing, and that's why I dropped one of the ivory pawns. It fell with a little sharp clatter on to the floor and rolled into a corner. I went after it and brought it back and set it down with enormous care exactly in the middle of its ebony square, and heard my own voice saying, 'Father, I've no wish to come into the business. I am for joining the Eagles.'

There was what seemed to be a very long silence, and a cart trundled past up the street from the docks, the mule driver swearing at his beast. Then my father said, 'Most of us are for joining the Eagles, at thirteen.'

'I'm nearly fourteen,' I said quickly.

'At nearly fourteen, then. It's a thing one grows out of.'

'It's not like that; I shan't grow out of it.' I was trying desperately to make him understand, but my father and I were never very good at making each other understand. I could find only one argument that I thought might carry some weight with him. 'Oh father, I'd make such a *bad* wine merchant, wanting all the time to be a soldier!'

But it was no use. He only leaned back and looked at me, putting the tips of his fingers together, as he did when talking business to someone across the writing-table in his office. 'We'll have to risk that, won't we? . . . My dear boy, the Legions are no life for anybody without wealth or influence to help them to the top. With all that I could give you of either, you might be a Centurion by the time you're my age; you'd certainly never be anything more.'

I said, 'I wouldn't want to be anything more.
Centurion Gavrus up at the fort isn't anything more
– and he's served in Gaul and Syria, and-and in
Dacia where the riders train their horses so that
they can jump them through a wall of fire. And
he's fought Nubian warriors on war elephants; and
he's got a long white scar all up his forearm – he
showed me – '

'Lucius!' My father stopped me in full spate,
making me suddenly feel as though I was about
four again, instead of nearly fourteen.

'Yes, father?'

'I know how wonderful all these things sound.
No doubt they would have sounded just as wonderful to me when I was your age. But there was a
place waiting for me in my father's business, and I
went into it. And later I came out and opened the
branch here in Britain, and settled down with your
mother, the Shades be gentle to her! *Now* there's
a place waiting for you in the business; and believe
me, Lucius, when you are my age, with a house
and family of your own, you'll be glad you took it,
instead of being on garrison service in some plague-
rotted camp at the other end of the Empire.'

I looked at his face, in the light of the palm-oil
lamp, and saw that it was pouchy and tired – the
kind of face business men often get when they eat
too much and work too hard but not with their
bodies. And suddenly I was sorry for him. But for
myself, I wanted all the more desperately to be a
soldier.

'So let me hear no more of this foolishness,' he said.

'But *father* – '

'One more word, and I shall begin to doubt the wisdom of letting you go up to the fort at all.'

'You couldn't be so – ' I began; but I saw the look in his eye, and I knew that he could. So I swallowed the rest.

'And now, shall we begin our game?' he said quietly.

So we played draughts. And I did not speak to my father again about joining the Eagles. Not that evening nor any other. Those visits to the fort meant too much to me to risk losing them. I just went on hoping, in my deepmost secret places, that one day something would happen, something, anything, so that I should be able to follow the Eagles instead of going into the place waiting for me in my father's business.

And the thing happened! Aye, it happened! But Name of Light! I never thought in those days what it would be!

*

It began the following year, with a rumour so small and seemingly unimportant that I can't remember even how I first heard it. It was just that the King of the Iceni had died – I'd heard vaguely of the Iceni, a big warlike tribe whose territory was far off in the great flat lands to the north-east – and having no sons, had left his kingdom divided between his Queen and our Emperor. I suppose he thought it would get better protection from other tribes that way than just left to a woman's rule. And better protection from Rome, too, may be. People laughed and said that the Emperor would have to turn horse-coper, if he wanted to make any use of his legacy, because the Iceni were horse-breeders to a man, with all their wealth in their stockyards.

And then there began to be other talk. I first heard it when I went with my father to the Bath House. All the men used to gather there as though it was a sort of club, and talk business and exchange news while they lay in the hot steam or strolled afterwards in the small colonnaded garden-court behind the cooling-off room. I'd only been into the plunge-bath and was out in the colonnade, sitting on the steps and waiting for my father to be ready to go home, when he and a couple of friends came strolling out into the evening sunshine. They were talking as they came, and so I missed the beginning of their discussion; but it wasn't hard to guess what they were talking about.

Kaeso the leather merchant said, 'And so she's giving trouble.'

'One of those turbulent women,' my father agreed. 'I doubt if anything will make her see reason.'

And Octavius Pudens, who dealt in worked silver and other precious things, shrugged his shoulders, 'Well, what can you expect? She is of the Iceni. She and her people follow the old ways.'

And then they had passed by, and two men came after them arguing loudly about the price of grain. And when they came back, the conversation had turned on to something quite different, and my father beckoned me to follow him, saying that it was time we were going home.

I did not like to ask him the meaning of what I had overheard; after all, he and his friends had not been talking to me. But once home, I carried the matter to Cordaella our house-slave, who had brought me up since my mother died. She was British – I mean, *still* British, not British by birth but Roman by adoption like most of my father's friends. She would know what they meant by 'The Old Ways'.

I found her in the kitchen, attending to the dish of milk-fed snails she was cleaning and fattening up for tomorrow's dinner. And I could see by her face as soon as I asked her that she did know, and also that it was something she did not want to talk about. But I had learned long ago that if I did not clamour, but waited quietly and showed no signs of ever going away, she would generally tell me what I wanted to know in the end.

There was a platter of little crisp honey cakes fresh from the hot charcoal on the cooking-hearth, and I took one, and sat myself on the corner of the table, eating it while I waited. Cordaella carefully tipped away the fouled milk in the snails' dish, and poured in fresh.

I helped myself to another honey cake and went

on eating. Cordaella set the dish aside. Then she looked up, slowly. 'Surely I know what they are, these "Old Ways". Among the Iceni it is the Queen who holds the life of the tribe in her hands, not the King. Prasutagus only ruled the Horse People because he was husband to the Royal Woman of the Tribe. The Kingdom was not his to leave.'

So that was it. It seemed a bit strange, just for the moment, but it was quite simple really. I nodded, still munching honey cake. 'I can see why she's angry, then. But I don't see there's much she can do about it.'

'She can refuse to yield up what your people demand,' Cordaella said.

'I suppose she could try – that's what they meant about her giving trouble. But Rome is stronger than she is.' I still did not really understand.

'Do you think so, little Roman fighting-cock?' A strange half-smile that was like a shadow brushed across her face. 'She is the Royal Woman. She is Epona the Mother of Foals, the Mother of All Things. She can raise the whole tribe.'

'One tribe against all Rome?' I said scornfully.

'All Rome is not here in Britain.' Suddenly Cordaella put her hands over her face, and her voice came like a stranger's, wailingly behind her fingers. 'Ayee! I see a red time coming!'

For that one moment, I remember, it was as though everything turned strange, and a little chill wind blew out of nowhere; then she became the old everyday Cordaella again, and dropped her hands.

'Na, na, I am a foolish old woman and I dream evil dreams. Go you and get ready for supper. I have put a clean tunic out for you.'

And the world swung back with her to its everyday self and grew familiar again.

But the Red Time came.

Perhaps if our officials had had more understanding of what they did, the story might have had a different ending; but – well, there's no denying that we Romans are not always very good at understanding the way that other people's hearts and minds work within them. So the Queen of the Iceni was harshly treated. She was in debt to Roman money lenders, and they had orders to call in the debt, knowing that after a bad foaling season, she could not pay. Some say she was even struck across the face by a Roman Officer during a quarrel (some say flogged, but the other seems more likely), and she and her daughters were driven, like troublesome camp-followers, out of the Royal Town. And so the Red Time came.

First we heard only rumours, washing and whispering to and fro through the city. And then the rumours hardened into news. The Iceni had swarmed out into revolt. The whole tribe was on the war-trail, with the Queen, Boudicca herself, leading them.

I mind it was a beautiful end-of-summer day, the last time I took the wine-cart up to the fort. The sort of day when you couldn't believe that all the world you knew was threatening to fall to pieces round your ears. . . . There had been a shower of rain in the night, just enough to lay the worst of the dust in the streets. And the swans were flying up-river. There were more people about even than usual; knots of them standing and talking with anxious faces at street corners; others had gathered around the temples or were drifting about not seeming quite sure where they were going or what they were going to do when they got there. And over everything, there was a feeling that was the beginning of fear, though it was not fear as yet. But still the sun shone, and the swans came with great slow wing-beats up-river.

I delivered the wine – six tall jars of red Falernian, the wooden stoppers clay-stamped with my father's own Capricorn seal, for it was good stuff meant for the officers' table. And then, leaving the mule hitched to a ring in the cookhouse wall, I went in search of my friend, Centurion Gavrus, hoping that he would not be too busy to talk to me.

I found him on his way to the gatehouse, where the great military road from the North came in. He grinned when he saw me, and checked, waiting for me to come up with him. 'The Light of the Sun to you, young Lucius. You're later than usual.'

'The city is very crowded today, and it took a long while to get through,' I told him. 'Like an ants' nest when you stir it up with a stick. It's all this talk of the Iceni.'

Gavrus gave a snort of laughter. 'Civilians! They

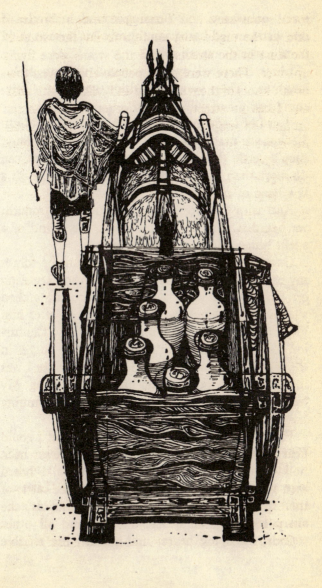

start squawking and running round in circles if one war-painted barbarian thumbs his nose at them from a week's march away!'

I was reassured by the scornful warmth of his laughter. 'Then you don't think anything – anything really *bad* will happen?'

'Lord of Light! what should happen? The Ninth Legion are marching south from Lindum already; they'll settle this Boudicca woman before she can do more than burn a couple of farms or drive off a few head of cattle.'

And with the words scarcely out of his mouth, we heard it. Far off up the road, the sound of a spent horse ridden at full gallop.

Gavrus' head went up. On the instant he forgot my existence and became very much the Centurion on Duty, as he went striding off into the arched shadow of the gatehouse. I wanted to go after him like a terrier at his heels, but even having a Centurion for your friend didn't make you free to get in the way of the Gate Guard. So I stood where I was in the sunlight, looking after him, and listening. My heart had begun to race in time with the drumming hooves, and my mouth felt very dry.

From where I stood, I could not see, but I could hear all that passed in the gateway, thrown back hollow-sounding by the arched entrance. I heard men turning out from the guardroom, the rattle of their pilum butts grounded on the cobbles, the sharp sound of an order, and, behind all other sounds, sweeping nearer and nearer, the terrible

uneven beat of that spent and stumbling gallop.
Then the horse was being reined in. I heard it
sobbing for breath. I heard the sentry's challenge:
'Who comes?'

And the rider's answer – by his voice, he was as
near to foundering as the beast he rode. 'News –
from Camulodunum – in Caesar's name.'

Then Gavrus' voice, clipped and clear, 'What
news, that travels at such a pace?'

'Death! It is the Iceni – They've burned Camulodunum – slaughtered every man, woman and
child – '

The last few words were growing blurred. Somebody said quickly, 'Look out! Catch him!' And
then I thought from the sounds that the messenger
must have pitched out of the saddle.

Two days later we heard that the Ninth Legion,
marching to head off the warhost, had been cut to
pieces.

That day the city seemed full of wailing, and
people cried out in the open street: 'The Gods have
pity on us!' And an old man sat on the steps of the
rams'-head conduit in Water Street, rocking to and
fro with dust on his head and crying out to the
passers by: 'The Gods have forsaken us! The Gods
have forsaken us!' until somebody hit him in the
mouth to stop his raven's croak.

We all knew by then that our one hope was
Suetonius Paulinus, the Governor General; he was
in the far west with the Twentieth and the Four-
teenth finishing off a campaign of his own when the

trouble broke. If he could reach us in time, we might be saved; if not. . . . Daily and hourly we waited for news – from the west – from the north. And while we waited, Suetonius brought his two Legions all across Britain by forced marches, and got to us ahead of Boudicca and her hordes.

Everyone was out in the streets to greet our Deliverer as he rode through the city with his escort to the Forum while his Legions waited outside the gates. I'd managed to get myself a good place on the roof of the Forum colonnade, over Bryn the sandal-maker's shop, close up to the Basilica itself, where I could see and hear all that went on. The whole Forum was a sea of people. They crowded round his horse as he rode through, and pressed in on him from all sides as he swung down from the saddle and mounted the Basilica steps to where the Chief Magistrate waited to greet him. But the cheek-guards of his helmet were pushed back; those that got nearest to him said afterwards that his face killed all hope in them before he spoke a word.

The crowd quietened as the Chief Magistrate held up his hand for silence, and I could hear every word. 'Sir, on behalf of myself and my fellow magistrates, and the Citizens of Londinium, I greet you and give thanks to the Most High Gods that you are come to our deliverance.'

Suetonius, beside him at the head of the Basilica steps, turned a little, to include the crowd in what he had to say. 'Magistrates and all people of Londinium, you must keep your greetings and your thanks; there is no time nor place for them here. I had hoped indeed to come to your deliverance. But I come only to bid you save yourselves as best you may. I cannot remain here to protect the City.'

I remember there was a moment of stunned silence all through that great crowd. Such a silence that, lost and lonely in it, I could hear the gulls crying down at the fish quay. And then the Chief Magistrate began, 'Sir – you cannot mean – '

Suetonius overrode him and the cries of protest that had begun to break out from that sea of people. His voice sounded hoarse and strained, but there was no yielding in it. 'The Ninth Legion is all but destroyed. Those that follow me now are more than two-thirds of the troops left in Britain. If I allow them to be penned up here, while we defend one city, the whole of Britain will go up in flames!'

The crowd were in an uproar now, pleading, cursing, praying. Just below me a woman screamed, her voice shrill and harsh above the tumult, 'General, for pity's sake – '

Suetonius heard her too, and glanced that way. 'I cannot afford pity. I need every trained man that I can lay my hands on; even the garrison of the fort I must take from you. The only advice I can give you is to get out of the City.' I saw how he was holding the whole crowd with his eyes, that tall, dusty man. 'Abandon your goods and gear; scatter as far and as fast as you can. Seek what shelter the forest can give you. I can give you none.' And then above the dreadful voice of the crowd, he cried out like a man in great pain and in a kind of fury: 'Do you think this is easy for me? A decision lightly taken? No more! In the name of all the Gods, *no more!*'

His staff officers closed round him, his escort thrusting back the people as he went heavily down the steps. Behind him he left the Magistrates looking oddly pitiful, as though they had been stuffed with sawdust, and some of the sawdust had leaked away. He remounted his horse, and then he was gone, forcing his way out from all the crying and the praying, and taking our last hope with him.

I dropped from the roof and made my way out through the rear of the sandal-maker's shop, and home by back ways. It was no good looking for my father in that crowd. All I could do was to go home and wait for him. I waited for what seemed a long time, sitting on the low wall of the little colonnade, and watching a pied wagtail darting after flies across the courtyard, and listening to the sounds that came in from the city. They were sounds of hurry and alarm, feet and cart-wheels and horses' hooves, all making one way, towards the river. The narrow timber bridge would be choked, and the boatmen would be able to ask any price they liked. But looking back, I doubt if they found much safety in the country round, those people who fled the city; for when the time came, the Iceni were everywhere for a while. . . .

My father came at last. I heard his footsteps across the atrium, and got up and turned to face him. And as he came out into the last of the sunlight, I remember noticing – it was an odd thing to notice at such a time – that his face looked harder and less pouchy than usual. He said: 'The news has just come in; they have burned Verulamium.'

I knew the place by name. It was on the great North road, nearer than Camulodunum. Our turn next, then. Outside, in the street, a trickle of people were still going by towards the river. We both heard them, standing there while the wagtail darted after flies on the sun-warmed roof and the familiar world crumbled and crumbled away. I didn't ask the question that was in my mind. But my father answered it as though I had.

'For myself, no. Everything I have, everything I am, is in this city; and even if I could, I'm too old to start all over again. I shall stay, and help to save Londinium if I can, and go down with it if I can't. But you – you're only a boy, Lucius; all your life in front of you. Get away if you can, and take my blessing with you.'

'I'm near enough a man to be able to use a spear,' I said. 'The Magistrates will give me a spear. I'll stay with you, Father.'

He stood looking at me a moment in silence, then nodded. 'They are opening the Armoury now; we'd best be getting up to the fort.'

'Not without warm cloaks,' said Cordaella's voice behind me, and when I turned round she was standing in the kitchen doorway. 'You will have a cold night's watch, I am thinking, for the wind has an edge to it, once the sun is down. Also, I have put some food together for you.'

I was so used to doing what Cordaella told me that I went to my sleeping cubicle without another word, and dragged my rough winter cloak out of the clothes' chest, and thrust the small native dagger that was my greatest treasure into my belt; and came out into the colonnade again. My father was already there, his cloak flung across one shoulder, and, a few moments later, Cordaella appeared from the kitchen with the food, bundled in a cloth. She put it into the hand my father held out for it, and I noticed that she did not bend her head in the accustomed way, but looked him full in the face as she did so, like a free woman.

I think a lot of slaves had run away by that time, but not Cordaella. I've wondered since, why not. I suppose she loved us, and it was as simple as that. . . . I suppose she had been a slave so long that there was no one else. . . .

I kissed her goodbye, and she put her hands on either side of my face and kissed me back. I knew I'd not be seeing her again – or our house. I remember taking a last look round our little courtyard, and noticing that the bay laurel looked as though it needed watering.

And then I went with my father up to the fort. I had never in all my life felt so close to him as I did that evening. It was another beautiful evening, the dregs of the sun westering up-river and the little chill wind that was rising brushing up the leaves of the poplars in the forecourt of the great temple to Diana until they showed moon silver. The whole city was at its fairest – I have noticed more than once, since then, that things sometimes have a special shine about them, just before they come to an end, like – oh, like something painted and garlanded for sacrifice. There were still a few people here and there making for the river, but most of those who were going had already gone; and the rest were heading, like us, for the fort.

The Magistrates were gathered there, and the Armoury had been opened. We received our few orders, and the weapons, left behind by the garrison, were given out to those of us who had none of our own. I remember the cold bright thrill that ran through me when I came forward to receive my spear. Such a child I still was, for all my talk of being a man! And before full darkness came down, we were in our places at the City gates and along the walls – wooden palisades they were in that first Londinium.

My father and I were among the main force set to guard the North Gate, not the one that came in through the fort, but the City Gate next to it, where the chief weight of the attack would most likely fall. I remember it as though it was something that happened an hour ago; men sitting and standing around the newly lit watch fires, leaning on their spears, and the flame-light on the waiting faces, merchant, goldsmith, baker, beggar. Behind us the City sounded empty. The women and children and any man too old or sick to be on the walls were huddled indoors or had crawled in to whatever hiding places they could find. Somewhere a dog barked and barked, and its barking became a howl. It might have been already a dead city.

And next day Boudicca and the warhost of the Iceni came down upon us.

Almost all that one ever knows of a battle – unless one is a general with a convenient hillock to watch from – is confusion and turmoil and the man at each shoulder and the man at the other end of your spear, who means to kill you if you cannot first kill him. That, and the smell of blood at the back of one's nose. So it was with me, that first fight of all. Just at first it was only the noise: the braying of British warhorns and the nearing thunder of hooves and chariot wheels and nothing to see but the blank gate timbers before my face. Then there came a rush of feet and a great shouting, and the first crash of the attack like a breaking wave set the gate timbers shuddering. My belly clenched itself and my hand was sticky on the spear butt. And then there was smoke everywhere, and red mares' tails of flame came leaping the stockades. 'Firebrands!' someone shouted. ' 'Ware firebrands!'

It had been a dry season – did I not say? – and the timbers of gates and palisades went roaring up like brushwood at summer's end, and everywhere the tribesmen came yelling in through the blazing gaps. We had built barricades behind the gates, but

they couldn't last long. My father went down beside
me, choking, with a tribesman's spear in his throat;
and the British chariots were thundering over the
blackened wreckage. . . .

I've seen my fair share of fighting since then, but
it's still that fight I dream of, when I eat too many
radishes for supper. Only it was not a fight, it was
a bloody massacre. They had scythe blades on the
wheel hubs of their chariots; and where the chariots
went, they cut red swathes. . . . But mostly, after
the first rush, they did their slaughtering on foot.
I was forced back, with a handful of others, down
the main street – I do not know how any of us lived
long enough to be forced back so far – right to the
portico steps of the Temple of Diana. All Londinium was burning round me. I saw a face that
was all eyes and snarling mouth; I saw the flame-
light in the eyes and on the blade of an upraised
sword; I saw a blackness laced with red, and heard
between me and the roar of fighting, a high, sweet,
terrible ringing in my head that ended in a crash
of silence.

When I came back to myself again, everything
was dark – no, grey, dawn grey – and the red
flamelight was all sunk away. Even the looting and
smashing and tearing apart must have been over;
all about me was the silence of death. I thought at
first that I was dead too; but when I tried to move,
the pain in my head told me that I was not. I
managed to get a hand up, and felt the dry blood
clotted on my forehead. People were lying on top

of me, all – very dead. I suppose that's what had saved me. It took me a while to struggle to my knees and then to my feet, but I managed it at last. And I was alive – just! – and I had only one thought in my swimming head: to get out of that dreadful dead city.

Somehow I found myself back at the North Gate – or rather, at the place where the North Gate had been. It was piled with hacked and hideous dead. I did not stop to look for my father's body among the rest. It would have been no use. I just crawled over them and kept on going. Outside the gate, I took the road to the North. Suetonius and the Legions had gone that way before the coming of the Killer Queen. And I followed the Legions; I followed Centurion Gavrus, I suppose. It seemed the only thing to do.

The countryside must have been swarming with raiding parties of the Iceni. I didn't know; I didn't even think about it. I lost the road and wandered pretty much in a circle. I didn't know that either. But truly the Fates must have meant that I should not die young for the next night, still, as I now know, within a few miles of Londinium, I came upon the Legions – just saw the red flicker of watch fires and blundered into one of their pickets.

A voice growled at me out of the darkness, and the firelight caught a levelled spear-blade in a way that brought the last moments of Londinium screaming back around my ears. 'Halt! Who comes?'

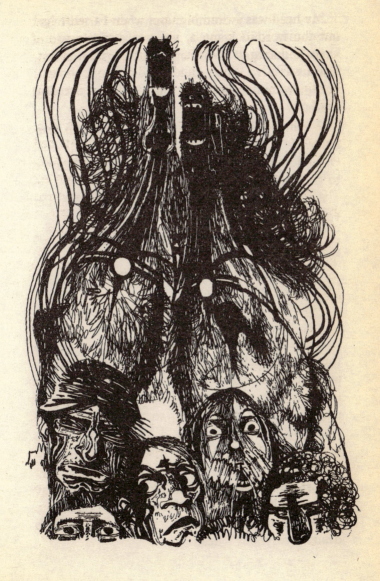

My head was swimming, and when I tried to get out the words I wanted, my tongue felt made of wool. I managed a sort of mumble, 'Centurion – Gavrus.'

'You're no Centurion,' the man said. I tried again.

'I want – Centurion Gavrus – Londinium Garrison.'

'Londinium – ' he began; and then as I started to go at the knees, 'Here – hold up, lad!'

An arm out of nowhere grabbed me, and another voice shouted, 'Sir!'

And I heard quick footsteps, and a clipped voice said: 'What is it, sentry?'

'This boy, Sir, asking for Centurion Gavrus of the Londinium Garrison.'

The officer said: 'And in pretty poor shape, too, by the look of him.'

His voice echoed in my ears, and went away into the strange high singing that I had heard before; and there was a sort of blink in time, and it was Centurion Gavrus bending over me, by the light of a spitting furze branch that somebody had pulled from the nearest fire. 'Yes, I know him,' he was saying. 'His father is – was – a wine merchant in Londinium.'

I let out a kind of croak as my head began to clear, and he bent closer: 'Lucius!'

'Londinium's dead,' I mumbled. 'My father's dead – everybody's dead.'

'Gods!' somebody said. They sounded sickened, but not surprised.

'So I've – come to join the Legions, please Gavrus.'

He had an arm round me, helping me to my feet. 'Time enough to talk of that later. The thing now is to get that gash in your head seen to. Steady! Steady, it's all right. . . .'

And that's all I remember for a while.

That was the night before the Killer Queen turned to fight. Suetonius Paulinus had chosen his place for bringing her to battle – only, like Londinium, it wasn't a battle, it was a massacre, but turned the other way round. The Iceni were over-confident. They must have felt that with their Goddess-Queen to lead them they could not fail; for I heard afterwards that they even drew up their supply wagons directly behind their own battle-mass, cutting off all hope of retreat if they should be forced back. And they *were* forced back – broken and driven back and cut to pieces against the wall of their own wagons.

The revolt was finished, and the Queen took poison rather than fall alive into our hands. Maybe she was wise.

Not that I saw anything of all that. I was lying in the back of one of our own supply wagons, with a bandaged head, not taking very much interest in anything just then.

Afterwards I served as a mule-driver with the

baggage train for a couple of years until I was old enough for the Legions. My father was perfectly right: I never rose beyond Centurion. But I've served under the finest General that the Roman Army has spawned in a hundred years, and I've a Distinguished Conduct bracelet to show for it, as well as a few scars – funny about that bracelet! The Second Augustan was my Legion, and our badge is a Capricorn, so the bracelet shows much the same device as my father used for sealing his wine jars. I'd never even thought of that – the badge, I mean – when I joined the Legion; it was just that it was the nearest, and Gavrus was serving with it at the time. (Centurions move about quite a bit once they get to Cohort rank.) But after the Legate had sprung the award on to my wrist, I went and sacrificed a cock to the Gods of the Underworld, for my father; I felt him again, for that moment, very near, as on the evening before Londinium fell.

Well, I always wanted to follow the Eagles instead of going into the wine trade. But dear Gods! I never thought how it would come about!

2

Rome Builds a Wall AD 123

Lucius Calpurnius, Senior Centurion of the Sixth Victrix, that's me. Lucius after my grandfather, who was the first of our family to follow the Eagles. *His* father was a wine merchant in Londinium, killed when Boudicca and her tribesmen sacked the city. My grandfather – he was only a boy at the time – escaped somehow, and hitched himself on to the nearest Legion (you know the rag-tag and bobtail that every Legion trails behind it). And, as soon as he was old enough, he joined up properly, in the Second Augustan. He served with Agricola on his great Caledonian Campaigns, and won himself a military bracelet for distinguished conduct: bringing off an ambushed patrol more or less in one piece and getting them back to the main body of the Legion. His most treasured possession, that bracelet was; but not for the obvious reason. He told me once that a Capricorn was his father's personal device, which he used for sealing the necks of his wine jars. And so, though this he never told me in so many words, I think he felt the broad silver band with its embossed Augustan Capricorn to be some kind of link with his father. A family thing as well as a military one.

At all events, when he came to die, he didn't have it buried with him according to the usual custom, but left it to me, my own father, his son, being already dead. So, it's mine now, and when my time comes, I shall hand it on to my son after me.

My grandfather and I were always good friends, and I remember well how, when I was a boy and eager for stories as most boys are, he used to tell me about those Northern Campaigns. Very bitter, he used to get, about the way Agricola was recalled to Rome with his work half done. 'We could have set our frontier on the Northernmost seashore,' he used to say. 'Nothing beyond it to the world's end. A frontier that would have been safe for all time. As it is, what have we?' And he'd start to rub his left thigh in the way that he had, where an old spear wound still ached when the wind was in the East. 'A handful of frontier forts strung out into the wilderness on supply lines so long and thin that they could be cut any dark night by three men and a boy with a dream and a blunt sword between them. Might as well build a wall across from Luguvallium to Segedunum and cut our losses north of it.'

Well, we've not cut our losses, we still hold our garrisons in Lowland Caledonia, though we had to let the Highland forts go. But after that last rising, when the whole of the North went up in flames and the re-formed Ninth Legion was lost without trace, we did build our wall.

Hadrian's Wall they call it now, because it was on the Emperor Hadrian's orders that it was built. Eighty-odd miles from coast to coast across the North of Britain. Seventeen forts, with mile-castles and signal towers between, and the Wall itself, striding along the high ground, stringing them all together into one great frontier line.

Oh, yes, I knew the Wall, knew it on winter nights when the sleet blows in your face as you pace the ramparts on sentry duty, knew it in green spring dawns, with the plover crying on the wind – there's always a wind blowing up there. Knew it with the distant hills a'swimmer in the August heat haze and the heather honey-scented and tall enough to hide a Pictish raiding party. Knew it before most of it was there at all, for I had a hand in building it. All three of the Legions in Britain had a hand in it, sending up each a couple of cohorts at a time. We've always been our own builders and road makers, we who follow the Eagles.

Anyway, there I was, just back from service in Germany, and newly promoted Centurion – young for it, too, though I says it that shouldn't – and my men behind me, tramp, tramp, tramping along the road towards Cilurnum at the day's end. Oh yes, the road was there already, looping along from hill-crest to hill-crest between the remains of an older frontier ditch and the new beginnings of the Wall. We came marching up the last slope into the eye of a low sunset, and checked before a timber gateway; and it's a proud man I was when I answered the sentry's challenge:

'Tenth Century, Tenth Cohort, Victrix. Detailed for Wall building duty!'

So the gate guard passed us through, and we marched into the big quarter-built fort, and grounded our spears before the row of wooden shacks that would be barrack-rows one day. And there we were at Cilurnum, more or less on the edge of nowhere. I went and reported to the fort commander, and next day, straight from the long march north, we started work.

It was the third working season, and the forts and mile-castles were beginning to take shape, and in places even the Wall itself was a course or two up from its foundations. Each Century worked on its own section; mine had the section running down to Cilurnum bridge where a river came out through the Wall from the North. Handy that was, because there was no bath-house up there as yet; and when the day's work was done, and we were hot and gritty from head to foot, with the stone dust even in our eyebrows, a plunge in the river was the next best thing to a proper bath.

The only trouble was that the fort's Asturian Cavalry, whose job was to guard us while we worked, came down to water their horses at about the same time.

It was a trouble I ran into on my very first day. We'd stripped off and taken to the water. Oh, but it felt cold and good on our hot, gritty hides! I was

plunging and rolling like a porpoise, my ears so full
of water and the sound of my own splashing that I
did not hear the trampling of horses' hooves and
the jink of accoutrements, until a bit of shouting
started, and I came up and shook the water out of
my ears and eyes, and saw the Cavalry Troop
among the alder and hazel scrub on the bank. The
shouting was going to and fro between them and
some of my own lads close inshore, and there
seemed to be a trifle of unpleasantness starting up.
So I waded ashore, and addressed myself to the
thick-set young man who seemed to be in command.

'What might be the trouble?'

He rounded on me, answering my question with
another: 'What, in the name of Hades, do you think
you're doing?'

'Taking a bath,' I said, scrambling up the bank.
I've often noticed that the simple truth annoys
people. It seemed to annoy him even more than he
was annoyed already.

'Upstream of the watering place! Do you expect
my horses to drink the water you've been washing
your filthy selves in?'

I grabbed at what dignity I could – which isn't
much, when you're stark naked and dripping wet,
and confronting a fully caparisoned cavalryman –
and said, 'Do you know who you're talking to?' or
something equally stupid.

He nodded. 'I saw you march in. You're the
new Centurion, and you command sixty men to my

thirty. Not, if I may say so, that it shows at the moment.'

Suddenly I began to get a glimmer of an idea that the thing was funny. 'If you'll just give me time to dry off and put on some clothes, maybe I can make a better showing.'

He said encouragingly: 'You do that, you put on your fine feathery helmet and I'll call you "Sir" and salute you; but meanwhile, call your lads off from fouling my horses' drinking water. There's all the river downstream for bathing in.'

'I do beg your pardon,' I said, 'I'm fresh from Castra Regina. We have baths there and no problem with the Cavalry drinking the bath-water.'

I found that I had begun to laugh. And he looked at me a moment, trying not to join in; then the corners of his mouth started to twitch and he gave up trying.

And that was how I made my first friend at Cilurnum. Felix, who commanded our single troop of Asturian Horse.

It wasn't long before I came to feel as though I'd been on the Wall since the day I was born. Life on the Wall has that effect on people. It's a life that gets into your bones. We did all the skilled work ourselves: shaping and dressing the stones, and making the mortar (an ugly job, working as we did, with unslaked lime, which is to say quick-lime, and slaking it afterwards. You get the hardest mortar that way, but if anything goes wrong and you get the foul stuff on your skin, you can end up dead or blinded as though by fire). And, of course, we did the actual building, with native labour teams from all the villages round to cart sand and gravel and bring up rough stone from the quarries; aye, and fell timber and work the lead mines under Roman overseers.

But I'm going too fast. I'd not been in Cilurnum much above a week when Centurion Marius Frontinus arrived on a visit of inspection. He was the Engineer-in-charge, and had his headquarters at Corstopitum, the big supply depot a few miles back from the frontier. But most of his time was spent moving up and down the Wall from coast to coast and back again, stopping a night or two at each fort, and keeping an eye on all things as he went.

I remember it well, too well for comfort, that first inspection after our arrival. We were working on the blockhouse at the Cilurnum end of the bridge. Getting the main walls up – inner and outer facings of cut stone, and, every time they go up another two or three courses, you pour liquid mortar into the space between, and pack the rubble filling down into it, and so on till you reach the top and the rampart-walk. It's quite simple really, but you can get air-pockets if you're not careful, and that weakens the structure. Well, so that's what my lads were doing; and along comes the fort commander, and Marius Frontinus with him, a little leathery man with an eye like an east wind that didn't miss much.

I gave him the salute, and would have stood my men to attention, but he made a quick movement of his hand for them to carry on, and fixed me with that east wind eye of his. 'Ah, Centurion, you're new since I was last this way.'

I said: 'We arrived nine days ago, Sir.'

He nodded: 'Done any building before?'

'Some of my men have. It's my first experience.'

'Thought so,' he said. His glance flicked once along the wall, and back to my face. And I had an uncomfortable and rather naked feeling that that single glance had probed out every nook and cranny of the building, and taken in every stone and every scrap of rubble and every joint in the masonry that might be a hair's breadth out of alignment, down to the deepest course of the footing. 'With experience you'll maybe learn to keep a more open eye on the work.'

I felt myself stiffen. 'Sir?'

'Take a look at that filling,' Frontinus said, pointing with his vine staff. 'Bit rough, isn't it?'

'I think it's quite sound, Sir.'

' "Think" isn't good enough. Soon see for sure,' he said; and raised his voice – it creaked like new harness leather. 'Crowbar here. Somebody break me a hole in that filling.'

I nodded to my senior optio to see to it; and, in a few moments, one of the men stepped up with the crowbar, and looked to me for the order. 'Get on with it,' I said; and he set to work.

We all stood round and waited, watching, not without anxiety, the hole that was growing in our nice new wall. All save Centurion Frontinus, that is, who seemed more interested in watching a buzzard as it spiralled, mewing, in sky-wide circles above us. Once, when the Legionary checked for an instant in his work with the crowbar, he brought his gaze earthward and said: 'Deeper, man, deeper,' and then returned to the wheeling buzzard. At last he was satisfied.

'So – that will serve. Now fill the hole with water.'

Another man brought up a slopping pail, and poured it into the hole; and again, we all stood by, waiting to see the water drain away into some badly packed hollow in the filling. It was one of the worst moments of my life. But the water stayed where it was. You could almost hear my men letting out their held breaths – me as well, come to that.

Frontinus said: 'No, seems sound enough. Right, fill in the hole. Carry on, Centurion!' and turned on his heel and walked away.

Telling Felix about it that evening, as we sat playing draughts in his quarters after supper, I was hot behind the ears with indignation. 'And not another word! Just strolled off and left me standing there like a corner stone – with an ugly great hole in my filling to be made good!'

Felix laughed, and moved a piece on the board. 'Did you expect him to apologize?'

'I'm not quite a lunatic! No, it was the *way* he did it, as though neither my men nor I were human beings.'

'Your move,' Felix said; and when I'd made it – it was a bad move and cost me the game – he reached for the jug of sour army-issue wine which was all one could get up on the Wall in those days, and refilled my cup. 'Have some more vinegar to drown your wrongs. . . . Oh, my Lucius, by the time you've been through a few more of his inspections, you'll have got used to the idea that our respected Chief Engineer cares much more deeply for corner stones and copings and well-cut ditches than he does for human beings.'

It was true in a way, I suppose; and yet – not altogether true. I remember one day towards the end of the working season, I rode over to the lumber camp with Frontinus. He had some trouble to settle with the native work team, the kind of thing you settle best, not by issuing a string of orders, but by going and talking to the chief man over a piece of bread and a pinch of salt. We rode south, dropping into the wooded valley where felling was going on at that time. The camp was pitched on the fringe of the trees, among the stacked trunks and white scars of newly felled scrub oak, and the faint haze of smoke hanging over brushwood fires. But well before we reached it, something rustled among the dun bracken and low-

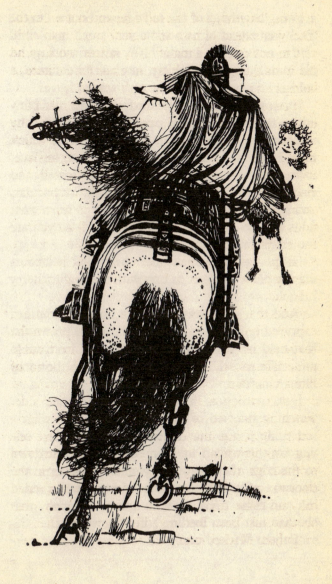

growing hawthorn of the hillside; and out on to the track just ahead of us burst a very small man-child clad in nothing but a rag of filthy saffron wool round his middle, and flourishing, in cheerful defiance, a wild cherry branch flaming with scarlet leaves.

Frontinus, who was nearest, swerved his pony aside, and stooped as he passed, scooped the baby up, blazing branch and all, and set it astride before him. It screwed round and looked up into his face, its mouth open, but too surprised even to yell, and Frontinus said gravely, speaking in the vernacular, and as man to man: 'It is always wise to learn what odds are too great for you to handle. Also you are too far from home.'

'Hup!' said the small one, cheerfully, belabouring the pony between its ears with the bright cherry branch.

'And that is no way to treat a horse.' Frontinus captured both the branch and the small brown fist that held it. 'Sit up straight and cease from wriggling like an eel, and you shall ride into the camp like a chieftain.'

I was riding a little behind and to one side, watching the two of them, and I thought what a sad thing it was that Felix would not believe one word of this when I told him. When we came down to the edge of the camp, a woman standing in the doorway of a branch-woven bothie saw us, cried out and came running, with a very new baby that she had just been feeding still at her breast.

'Baban! Wicked one!'

'This is yours?' Frontinus said. 'We found it halfway up the hill. It tried to get itself killed under my horse's hooves, you should not let it stray so far from home.'

'Stray! he is for ever straying – the moment that my eyes are off him. And now that there is the new one to see to – ' She put up her free arm to take the child as Frontinus stooped from the saddle to give him to her, and let him slither to the ground, where he slipped behind her and stood peering out at us from the shelter of her skirts.

'Truly, my thanks are to your honour for bringing the bairn home to me,' she said. She was in rags, with her hair – it would have been bright as new-minted gold had it been clean – hanging in wisps out of its careless braids; but, like all her kind, she had the manners of a Queen to use when she chose. And Frontinus made her the gesture of courtesy that he would have made to a fine lady. No, I think he would probably *not* have made it to a fine lady. It was for her and the man-child clinging to her skirts and the small brown baby she was still feeding. I saw his face, and for a moment there was a look on it that I could not read, or that passed before I had time to read it. And we rode on into the camp.

It was evening when, with the trouble that had brought us sorted out, we rode back over the high moors towards the Wall. The bracken and haw-thorn scrub of the lower slopes had given place to heather that was almost over, a dark tide of heather making a dry hushing sound about our horses' legs, and one or twice a starring of faded harebells in the shelter of a lichened stone. Ahead of us, drawing nearer, the Wall flung its giant strides along the crest of the land, and again there was the haze of smoke, from evening cooking-fires this time, rising from the fort and the labour camp to the south of it.

Frontinus, who had been very silent, sniffed like a hound. 'Smell of frost in the air. Soon be time to shut her down for the winter.'

'We've got a good season's work done, Sir,' I said.

'Not so bad; not so bad at all. Nothing to spare, mind you. It's the third season, and the Emperor's orders are to finish in five.'

We rode on, in silence again, no sound but our horses' feet brushing through the heather, and the soughing of a little thin wind that had begun to rise, and the walls of the fort rising higher and darker as we drew towards it. And then, as though there had been no break, Frontinus said, 'And what will you be doing with your well-earned winter leave?'

'Head south and see a bit of life at Eburacum,' I said. 'I might even try for a look at the bright lights and fleshpots of Londinium if I get long enough to make it worth the trip – and you?'

He did not answer for a moment. Then he said: 'Don't suppose I shall take much leave. There are always the lumber camps and the quarries to keep an eye on, even when work stops on the Wall itself. . . . And I'll have all the leave I want – more – all the leave in life, when the next two seasons are over.'

Something in his voice made me glance aside at him, but his leathery face was shut, and there was nothing in his eyes but the distance and the fading daylight. And yet I felt – I don't quite know what I felt, but it came to me suddenly what the future must look like to a man of Frontinus' kind when he had laid his last road and built his last fort. And I knew that I couldn't just leave the thing lying there.

I began awkwardly: 'You mean – '

'I'll be due to retire, yes. I've built a good few roads and bridges, and drained a marsh or two in my time. But the Wall is my last job before I take my wooden foil.'

I said: 'It's a good sizeable one.' It sounded stupid and obvious, but it was the best I could do.

'Aye,' he said. 'Something to think about, while I rust out at Aquae Sulis or another of those pleasant little towns in the South that my kind retire to.'

And I, I was stricken suddenly with pity, which isn't the kind of thing you expect to feel for a man like Marius Frontinus, and I didn't quite know what to do about it. To cover up, I said quickly and lightly: 'There should be plenty to think about, at all events; it's said along the Wall that you are personally acquainted with every stone of it from one end to the other.'

'And with every foot of filling, eh?' he said with a flicker of amusement, and we rode on again in silence. We were almost into the Wall workings when he broke it again, abruptly, and looking straight between his horse's ears. 'There was a time once, I thought I'd have other things – people – to fill the gaps after my time with the Eagles was through; but that was long ago when I was young. She – died when the child came, and took it with her. . . . I suppose, lacking wife or children, you make do with the job, and it grows to take their place. But when the time comes for your wooden foil, you have to leave the job behind. . . .'

And so we rode into camp, without another word.

I've wondered often enough since what made him open up like that, just once, and to me whom he hardly knew. It could have been the urchin down at the lumber camp and the urchin's mother with the new baby. Smaller things have toppled empires before now. The moment came, and passed, and it happened to be me that was riding beside him; that's all I know.

Well, that season ended and the next one came, and we got the main part of the fort built round ourselves, and also a bath-house south of it among the scatter of turf and timber bothies that were beginning to spring up like toadstools round an old tree stump. You know how it is, wherever there's a Roman fort a town of sorts springs up in the lea of it. Stables and granaries and little streets of merchants and craftsmen and temples to a score of Gods and the bothies where the Legionaries keep their women and families and kennel their hunting dogs.

Not that there was all that at Cilurnum *then* you understand; but it was beginning. That season an ex-Legionary applied for permission to open a wine-shop. And a British bronzesmith set up his smithy, making the kind of harness extras and ornaments that the cavalry like but the army doesn't provide as regulation issue. We had begun to be a trading post, too, where merchants from the south met hunters down from the north with wolf and bear and mountain-fox skins for sale. Then there was the usual trade in hounds and fighting-cocks – horse-coping, too. The men north of the Wall used to come down from time to time with small sturdy hunting ponies to sell among the frontier garrisons. Felix and I got to know one of them quite well, a little, bow-legged, red-headed devil called Conn. . . .

I mind coming up with him one day, standing straddle-legged and head back beside one of the big cranes, watching it as it hoisted the squared blocks of stone to the top of the Wall, where the course-setters waited to receive them and set them in position.

'Truly, this is a marvel, this great hoisting-wheel, when one looks at it closely,' he said. 'It is small wonder that the Romans, who can make such

things, are the masters of the world and of all ignorant barbarians such as we.'

'Small wonder indeed,' Felix said. 'But let us
agree that you are looking at it somewhat too
closely. You see that block of stone swinging up
there? If the rope slips, you are going to be not
only one ignorant but one very dead barbarian.'

Conn made his eyes wide and innocent. 'But
assuredly no rope made fast by the Romans would
ever slip.'

'Assuredly not,' Felix said. 'But come now and
show us what beasts you have brought with you
this time.'

He took us across to where half-a-dozen ponies
were tethered, rumps turned to the fine rain that
was beginning to drive from the south-west. 'I have
a red mare – here – sure-footed as a mountain stag,
if my Lord is interested.'

Felix walked all round the mare, slowly, wrink-
ling his nose. 'Hmm,' he said at last. 'Better try
selling her to the Centurion Lucius. He doesn't
know as much about horseflesh as I do.'

I was rubbing the mare's nose. I could see that
she was inclined to be hammer-headed, but she
was sound enough in most ways. But on a junior
Centurion's pay, you don't buy a second pony that
you don't really need. 'Thanks, no,' I said. 'From
the look of her, I'd say you're needing to get fresh
blood to improve the breed.'

Conn was righteously indignant. 'Can I help it

that you Romans come and build a wall right across – '

'Right across your raiding grounds,' I said. 'Oh yes, we all know that you used to spend half your time raiding into the Brigantian runs.' I gave the mare a final pat on her nose. 'But they spent the other half raiding into yours, remember.'

Conn said regretfully, 'It kept the young men fit for the war-trail. Aiee! – those were good days; the Wall has spoiled many things.'

Felix gave a splutter of laughter. 'Why, you wicked old horse-thief!'

And then the trumpet sounded for watch setting, and I had to hurry, for I was due back on duty.

But I wish I knew if it was that small exchange over the red mare that first put the devilry into his head – a sort of challenge – or whether it was there already. I hope it was there already. But no one can ever know now. . . .

The next evening, Frontinus rode in on one of his visits of inspection. And a foul evening it was, too, with half a gale from the south-west driving grey swathes of rain across the moors, the sort of weather when you can't see a Pictish war-band half a bow-shot away. (Not that you ever see a Pictish war-band anyway, until it's on top of you!)

The only bright spot anywhere was that Sextus, one of the Senior Centurions, had been out hunting a few days since, and the stag he had killed was just ripe for eating, so there would be a good supper in Mess that night.

But I did not eat in Mess that night. I was Duty Centurion. When you're Duty Centurion for the night, you spend a good deal of it doing rounds; and, in between whiles, you sit with your drawn sword on the table before you, in the little lighted room – the Sacellam we call it – where the Cohort Standard and the pay chest are housed; and you eat your supper there too, in solitary state. Well, so I did First Rounds, and ate my solitary share of Sextus' kill, and began to write up the reports and such that always fall to the Duty Centurion's lot.

Except for the pacing steps of the sentry that came and went along the colonnade outside, there was nothing to be heard but the wind and the rain. I might have been alone in a dead fort, with nothing moving, save the ghosts when the draughts set the lamp-flame jumping. And then the trumpet sounded for the second watch of the night, and I turned the hourglass, and presently it was time for Second Rounds.

I got up and slammed my sword into its sheath, flung on my cloak, and went out. The wind and rain swooped into my face as I slammed the Sacellam door behind me, and passed the sentry outside. Night Rounds, especially in rough weather, have a strangeness about them, a great loneliness, that is in some way akin to the loneliness of the Mysteries. Indeed I have felt much the same thing in the Bull Cave during the Raising Ceremony, as though one had come to some borderland between this world and another; but one is not sure whether it is oneself or the sentries challenging out of the stormy darkness, who are the ghosts.

I made my way from guardpoint to guardpoint, sentry post to sentry post; at each one, the alert movement of a shadow in the night, the sound of a pilum butt grounded in salute.

'Who comes?'

'Duty Centurion. All's well?'

'All's well, Sir.'

And the exchange of the password for the night.

And then on again, to the next point, and the next, and the next.

Lastly, that night, huddling my cloak round my ears, I made my way out along the line of the Wall towards the bridge. The blockhouse was not properly finished yet, but we kept a guard there, because the iron grills for closing the space under the bridge were not yet fixed, and until that was done it was a weak place in the defences. The blockhouse made a square of blackness against the shifting lesser dark of the river and the storm-drenched night. There was a glimmer of torchlight from an open doorway, and again the sentry's challenge.

'Who comes?'

'Duty Centurion. All's well?'

I shouldered in for a few moments' shelter by the fire. The blockhouse was a shell of warmth and light, the dark and the storm pressing in on all sides.

'What a night!' someone said.

'It certainly isn't the kind you'd expect to find anyone abroad on – except maybe the Wild Hunt.'

And at that very instant, between gust and gust of the wind, we heard the high protesting squeal of a scared horse, coming as it seemed from almost under our feet.

In the torchlit guard-post men looked at each other in a split moment of utter stillness lapped round by the tumult of the storm. Then the sentry was in the doorway. 'Horses, Sir – under the bridge.'

I nodded: 'After me, all of you – quick.'

Then we were outside and crouching in the lea of the blockhouse wall, with the steep drop of the bank below us, and the water running yeasty under the bridge. And against the yeastiness of the water, half-blinded as I was by the rain, I could just make out a movement of dark shapes. There was a splashing and a trampling of horses, and a muffled curse. I drew the Optio back to the corner of the blockhouse. 'Ulpius, get back to the fort, and report horse-raiders trying to break through under the bridge. Trumpeter – sound the alarm! The rest of you, out swords and follow me!'

And as the trumpet brayed, the high notes teased out and flung away by the wind, we went plunging down to the attack. The raiders met us at the water's edge. We fought among the storm-lashed alders on the bank; we fought in the water itself, the horses swirling and plunging about us before they broke away. It was a small, vicious struggle, confused as a fight in the ragged end of a dream: a flurry of slash and stab in the dark. I was caught in a tangle of blows with somebody, a black shadow like all the rest, until a gleam of light from the block-house showed me his face for an instant as we reeled to and fro. And it was Conn!

I shouted, 'Conn! *You!*'

And he laughed, and shouted back: 'Did you not say we needed fresh blood to improve the breed?' His blade slashed past my cheek and turned on my shoulder-piece (the metal had to be beaten out afterward, and I carried the mark for many a long day) and he slipped in the mud, and my point took him under the collarbone as he went down.

That was pretty near the end of it.

They might have got through, if that one horse hadn't taken fright and squealed. As it was, well, the Quarter Guard was down to our help and the thing was over before it was well begun. And our lads were rounding up the scattered horses, and Conn and a couple more of the tribesmen were sprawled dead on the river bank, and the rest had got away.

I heard the voice of the Senior Centurion somewhere, lifted above the storm. 'Let them go, we've got the horses.'

But I didn't take much notice. I was squatting close under the blockhouse wall, where there was

a little shelter from the wind and rain, with the Chief Engineer propped against my knee. Someone had brought a torch, and we could see that there wasn't anything to be done. He'd taken a stab wound between the ribs – he had no harness on, no protection but his leather tunic, just as he'd come from the Mess table – and was bubbling blood with every breath he drew.

'Gods!' someone said. 'It's Frontinus!'

I nodded.

'What in the name of the Black One did the old fool want to get mixed up in this lot for?'

Frontinus looked up at us with a flicker of humour. 'Would you have – had me sit on my rump in the – fort, while a mob of misbegotten horse-thieves cut the picket lines and – broke out through – *my Wall*?'

'Your Wall!' I said furiously. I think I was weeping.

'*My Wall*.' Frontinus' voice was going, and I had to bend close to catch what he said above the tumult of the storm. 'Someone else will – have to finish it. But – it will be a good wall – all the same!' He tried to laugh. 'Ah, now, never look so woebegone! Better this way than – slowly – rusting out at Aquae Sulis – after all!'

He gave a small wet choking sound, and his head fell sideways against my shoulder.

I laid him down and got to my feet. I gave the necessary orders, and by and by I went back to the

Sacellam, and fell to cleaning my sword, which was red when I laid it on the table.

We finished building the wall Hadrian had ordered, but under a new Engineer. I don't suppose many people remember Frontinus now, except those of us who served under him, and our ranks are thinning as the years go by. But his Wall will stand while Rome lasts. Maybe longer!

Felix and me? Felix has done well. He's praefect of an Egyptian Legion, these days. I've never got beyond Senior Centurion. Lacked ambition, I suppose, like my grandfather. Besides, I married a British girl, and lost the taste for marching around the Empire in search of glory.

3
Outpost Fortress AD 150

Let me present myself: another Lucius Calpurnius, another of us following the Eagles. But I'm the first of us to do so on horseback instead of on foot. When you have the kind of short bow-legs that look as though you'd been born on a horse, to join the Cavalry seems the obvious thing to do.

I almost *was* born on a horse. At least, I was astride one before I could walk steadily without clinging to my nurse's finger. My father bred good horses on our farm in Southern Gaul. He was invalided out of the army with an arm crushed in a catapult accident before I was born, and settled in my mother's country. So I was born and bred in the South, and my trees were the pine and olive, and my sea the Mediterranean, and I never saw Britain until I was posted to Trimontium, away north of Hadrian's Wall, to take over the lead of a troop of Dacian Cavalry. It's odd the way we keep on coming back to Britain, in our family. We mostly serve here at one time or another, and some of us settle here when we retire – if we live long enough to retire and settle anywhere – and those of us who go elsewhere mostly send our sons back in our stead. I had a British grandmother.

The day my posting came through, my father sent for me to his study. And when I went in to him, he was standing at his writing-table, holding the family bracelet, turning it in his good hand and looking at it as though it was something he had never seen before. It's just an ordinary silver military bracelet embossed with the Capricorn badge of the Second Legion, the kind of thing they hand out for distinguished conduct, but of an outdated pattern. It was earned on one of Agricola's Caledonian Campaigns by the first of our family to follow the Eagles, and, for some unknown reason, it wasn't buried with him in the usual way. It's been a family treasure ever since.

My father was never one to waste words in leading up to anything. He looked up as I entered, and held it out to me: 'Ah, Lucius, I think the time has come when you should take charge of this.'

I stood and looked from his face to the Capricorn bracelet and back again, too surprised for the moment to make any move. 'Our bracelet? But why, Father?'

'You're my eldest son, and it will be yours after me in any case,' he said. 'But since you are going back to Britain, and up North, beyond the Wall at that, it seems to me right and fitting that you should have it now, to take with you.'

'I'm in no hurry, Sir,' I said. 'I'll wait.'

'Until it comes to you in my will? No, it's time it saw active service again. I used to wear it when I was a young man, for – oh, I don't know, for luck, I suppose. At all events, I wasn't wearing it on the day the catapult keeled over on to me. Pushed well up under the sleeve of one's tunic, it doesn't show.'

I still hesitated. And he smiled, a smile of the eyes that barely touched his mouth. 'Take it – with my love.'

So I took it (the silver was warm where he'd been holding it) and sprang it on to my arm, pushing it high up under the sleeve of my tunic. The silver band had been forced open, making it too big to wear in the usual place on one's wrist; it was odd that I had never thought about that before. The bracelet felt good, from the first. The right feeling of something that belongs.

Something over six weeks later, I stood facing my new Cohort Commander across another writing-table, in his quarters in Trimontium that the British call 'The Place of Three Hills'.

He was sitting forward with his arms folded on the table, and surveying me in a way that made me want to scuffle my feet; it was so obvious that he was coolly taking my measure while he talked. He said: 'The Seventh are a fine troop, and if you can earn their trust and their respect, they'll follow you through fire and flood, but you're not going to have an easy time of it meanwhile.'

'Sir?' I said.

'They're a fine troop, as I said, but they're renowned for being difficult to handle, and they had great personal loyalty to Valarius, their last Decurian.'

'What happened to him, Sir?' I asked, rather anxiously. It seemed to me this might have a good deal of bearing on my chances with the Seventh. If I was taking the place of a man transferred under a cloud – anything of that sort. . . .

'He died of fever.'

'At least, they can't hold me accountable for that, Sir,' I said hopefully.

'When you have lived in this unjust world as long as I have,' said the Commander, 'you will have learned that it is quite surprising, the things that one man – still more a group of men – can hold another accountable for. Furthermore, it so happens that until now, the Seventh have always had a Dacian leader. They're going to give a rough ride to any officer following Valarius, but especially to one who isn't from Dacia!'

'I'll do my best, Sir,' I said.

'Naturally.' He unfolded his arms and took up one of the muster rolls lying on the table, to show that the interview was over. 'Good luck to you, Decurian.'

'Thank you, Sir,' I said, and gave him my best salute, though he wasn't looking. As I turned and marched out past the sentry on the door, I was thinking that by the sound of things, I was going to need it. I thought also, half laughing at myself, half in earnest, that I was glad my father had given me the family bracelet, after all.

Once you know the pattern of garrison life in one corner of the Empire, you know it in all the corners there are, from a mud fort on the Nile to the big Northern Frontier Outpost of Trimontium. It's a four-square life, ruled by the trumpets sounding for watch setting, for meal times, Lights Out and Cock-Crow, a constant succession of patrols out and in, camp fatigues, parade-ground bashing, weapon-practice – and, by way of a change, escort duty with the supply train, or turning out a guard of honour for some visiting general. Not often much fighting, except in some newly formed outpost, but always enough chance of it to keep one's sword sitting loose in its sheath. . . .

The fort itself follows much the same pattern from end to end of the Empire, too – the same four gates, and two straight streets, with the Praetorium, the official buildings and officers' quarters, where they cross each other in the middle. The same lines of workshops and store-sheds, armouries and bar-rack rows, and the horse lines if it's a cavalry fort.

Trimontium is a double fort, infantry and cav-alry: a regular legionary cohort, and the Dacians.

I fitted into the life of the fort easily enough. But number Seven Troop! At first, before I had had time to get the 'feel' of things, I thought all was well there, too; and it took me a few days to learn my mistake! Well, I couldn't complain that the Commander hadn't warned me. Oh, they didn't disobey orders! – well, no more than all soldiers do if they get the chance. They carried out their camp duties as efficiently as any other troop of the Cohort, and they were good enough on patrol. (We did a lot of patrol work, keeping an eye on the country round.) No, they specialized in Respectful Hostility. They were experts at it. Never anything you could lay a finger on. They would talk among themselves in the tongue of their own tribe, whenever they knew that I was within hearing; and when I spoke to them in Latin, which they spoke and understood as well as I did, they gazed at me with blank faces, and asked, 'Will you to say again, Sir – slowly, please.'

They called me 'Sir' with just a shade too much respect to ring true, and they looked at me with something shut behind their eyes, and I never knew if I would be able to rely on them in any kind of tight corner. They took very good care that I should not, very good care that I should not know anything about them at all, even whether they were going at any moment to blossom into open warfare.

It didn't help that one of the first things I had to do was to bring Trooper Pertinax up before the Commander for being drunk and disorderly, and he got seven days cleaning out the latrines.

Trooper Pertinax spent a good deal of his time cleaning out the latrines for being drunk and disorderly, or for breaking camp to court a girl in the town outside, or for letting his equipment get rusty. He was very popular; his sort – 'Emperor's Hard Bargains', they're called in the Legions – generally are, and, give him a bit of charred stick, he could draw pictures fit to make a cat laugh. So, as I say, running him in to the Commander didn't help. . . .

Well, time passed, and one day in late summer we heard that the Legate was coming up from Eburacum to inspect the frontier defences. He was a new man, and we all know about new brooms sweeping clean! He was to spend two days at Trimontium; and it was arranged that on the first day he should inspect the fort, and watch the legionaries building a wall and then taking it by assault – all the kind of stuff soldiers hate – and on the second day, the Dacian Horse should entertain him with cavalry manoeuvres. Pertinax was doing another spell in the latrines for a really monumental piece of drunken insubordination that had finished up with spitting on the Duty Centurion's feet. But he would be out in time to take his place with the rest of Number Seven, which was a relief, because he was one of the best riders in the troop.

The blunt-tipped spears and great masked and plumed parade helmets were issued to us, and we got down to some hard practice. That was when I nearly became insane. The troop managed somehow to give the impression that they were doing their best but had genuinely forgotten how to keep station or tell their left hands from their right. They kept that up for the whole of the first day, and we only had four. On the morning of the second, I rode in front of them, and said, 'See, my children, and listen: surely the Decurian Valarius cannot have trained you so badly that in the five months I have led you, you have lost all that he put into you, as well as all that your Dacian breeding put into you before ever you were born? Do you wish so much to shame me before the Legate, that for the sake of doing so, you will shame not only the dams that bore you, but the Decurian Valarius?'

I looked along the lines, and they sat their fidgeting horses and looked back. But I saw my words sink in. It was the first time I had seen anything behind their faces. That day they worked well and hard, and I thought that I was winning.

I should have known better.

That evening, just before the Dismiss, with the whole troop looking on, my Second came to me with a suggestion. For the moment he had given up the pretence that he could not speak Latin. This was a more serious thing altogether.

'Sir, I was wondering if we could not do something to make these manoeuvres a bit – different.'

I said, 'Such as?'

'If you got the Commander's leave, Number Seven could do a Fire-ride.'

'A Fire-ride!' I felt them all watching me, and kept my voice level.

'Yes, Sir. It's quite a common trick, we've all done it, back home in Dacia; but it's spectacular to watch, and it looks more dangerous than it is. You have a hedge – three hedges to make a really good show – of blazing brushwood, and gallop the horses through the flames. *These* horses would have to be blindfolded because they haven't been trained to it.

But one treats their hides with a brew of certain herbs so that they don't scorch. They're perfectly safe.'

I said, 'And the men?'

'Well, of course we don't treat our own hides, that would spoil things. But it's safe enough for the men, too, so long as they don't hesitate, and don't breathe at the wrong moment.'

He kept his eyes fixed on mine, bright and cool, and the rest stood round with their arms through their horses' bridles, waiting to see how I took to the idea.

'I could show you the way of it easily enough, Sir,' said my Second. 'Or of course, if you had rather, I could take them through *for* you, *Sir*.'

My mouth felt uncomfortably dry. I suppose most of us have some special private fear of our own. Mine had been of fire, ever since the day that I was trapped in a burning hay-loft when I was six, and only rescued just in time. They couldn't know that. I wonder if it would have made any difference if they had. 'If we do this ride, naturally I lead,' I said. 'Can we get the herbs to protect the horses hereabouts?'

'Easily, Sir.'

'Carry on, then Number Two.'

And I went to the Praetorium to ask leave of the Commander.

I found him in his quarters, just about to change for supper. But he sat down and listened to my request.

'A Fire-ride,' he said, when I'd done. 'Yes, it makes a fine showing. I've seen it done more than once when I was stationed in Dacia. Very well – Your Second will lead, of course?'

'No, Sir,' I said, 'I lead.'

He cocked his head in a way that he had when he was surprised or interested. 'So? You've never done it before?'

'No, Sir.'

'Can you do it?'

'I must,' I said, hoping my voice didn't sound as desperate to the Commander as it did to me, 'if I don't, I'll never command them – and they know it as well as I do.'

There was an odd look – an odd mixture of looks – on his face. He understood the seriousness of the thing to the full, and at the same time he was deeply amused. 'The fiends!' he said, very softly. 'The – *fiends!*' And then, 'Very well, permission granted. Lead your Fire-ride, Decurian!'

I remember, as I came out from his quarters, touching the old silver bracelet that I wore high under my uniform sleeve, rather as one touches a talisman for luck. I'd a feeling I was going to need all the luck I could get. . . .

That evening I went down to the Four Pigeons just outside the main gate of the fort. Two other troop leaders were there already, sprawling at a table in the corner; the Cavalry mostly tended to gather at the Four Pigeons, while the Legionaries did their drinking and cock-fighting at the Golden

Gladiator. They made room for me, and we sat together for a while with a jug of wine between us, talking over the manoeuvres and rather idly playing dice. Then another man came strolling across to join us. The Decurian of Number Five Troop. Long elegant legs, he had. I'd never liked him, even then.

'What, Florianus?' Androphon said. 'Trust you to hear the rattle of the dice if you were at the other end of the Empire!'

Florianus hitched up a stool and sank down on it. 'Dear Androphon, how I wish I was! Fugh! These northern summers! Let's have some more wine to warm ourselves up, I've had a present from my father.' He lifted up his voice, 'Hi! Boy! More wine here!'

And we drank again; presently, without quite knowing how it happened, I was casting the dice with Florianus.

I had Ahriman the Black One's own luck that night. Again and again I threw the Dog, the lowest throw of all, while Florianus' luck was as far in as mine was out. It was fortunate – very fortunate for me that night – that along the frontiers, where few of us had more than our pay to live on, we seldom played for high stakes. But I could not remember that evening's play more vividly if we had been dicing for a kingdom. I remember Florianus' face in the lamplight, smiling a little, with narrowed eyes, and the rattle of the dice in the wooden cup, and his hand spilling out fours and fives and sixes across the wine-stained table.

I don't know how long we played, but it must have been a good while later that he made the final throw of a game, and laughed softly. 'Aha! Venus! The Treble Six! Shall we play again?'

'Not tonight,' I said. 'You've about cleaned me out.'

He gave a small shrug. 'How sad! And I had a feeling your luck was just on the turn.'

I looked at the three sixes lying on the table, and they seemed to stare back at me with all of their eighteen malicious little black eyes. 'I'm afraid I've lost count. How much do I owe you?'

'Not much. Six hundred sesterces I make it.'

I had indeed lost count – oh, it wasn't very much! Less than half the price of a good native pony or an untrained slave. At the start of the month, I could have paid it and got through till next pay-day by tightening my belt. But it was near the end of the month, and my purse was low.

I was ashamed. I said: 'I'm sorry. I can give you two now, and the rest next week when I get my pay.'

He said in a voice as soft as silk, 'Has no one ever told you that it is usual to pay a gaming debt before leaving the table?'

Before I could answer, Androphon at my side put in quick and kindly, 'Look, I've a bit put by; I'll settle for you now, and you can pay me back next week.'

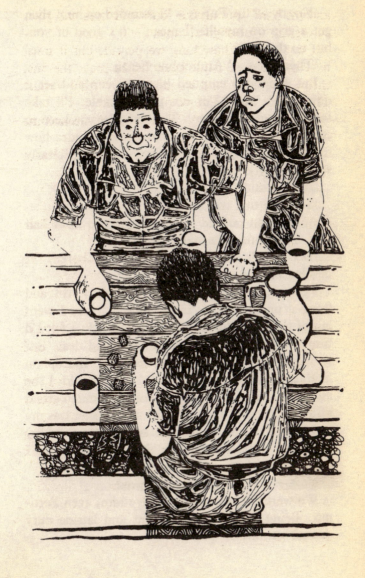

'No, by all the Furies – ' I rounded on him, then got a grip on myself. 'I mean – it's good of you, but no thanks.'

'Then what – ' Androphon began.

But Florianus emptied his wine cup and set it down. 'See now, I'm not unreasonable; I'll take something else in surety. That bracelet you keep so carefully up your sleeve – have you any idea how much it shows when you raise your arm? It's clearly something you value.'

'It is,' I said.

'So, then that will serve.'

Androphon pushed his own wine cup away half full. 'Florianus, you make me sick!'

'Do I?' Florianus sounded faintly bored. 'It desolates me to hear it.'

I got up, dragging the bracelet from my arm, and flung it on the table. 'Here, take it.' And I went out of the Four Pigeons, also feeling sick. I felt I'd brought dishonour on something I held dear. But it would have been worse to have let Androphon lend me the money. Also – why should I be ashamed to admit it? – I was still very much afraid of that accursed Fire-ride, and the bracelet was my luck, my talisman against disaster. A bunch of my own men were lounging by the door, and after I was past, I felt them turn to look after me.

Next evening, the Legate arrived.

We were all paraded to receive him, even Pertinax. Being confined to barracks and latrine duty doesn't get one off parades.

So there we were, all drawn up along the Praetorian way. Horse and Foot, all trying to look as
much as possible as though we were carved out of
wood. There was a great barking of orders, and,
then, with the trumpets sounding the Salute, he
came jingling through the gateway and up between
our lines, with his escort, also jingling, behind him.
Inside his fine gilded bronze, he was a surprisingly
little man. His eagle-crested helmet seemed too big
for him, and when he dismounted, I swear by the
Lord Mithras, his legs were bandier than mine!

I mind when he'd passed out of hearing, there
was a breath of laughter somewhere behind me,
and under pretence of stilling a fidgeting horse,
someone whispered to a neighbour: '*He* should have
joined the Cavalry too!'

Next day our new Legate made his Inspection of
the Fort. I was one of those ordered to go round
with him – I think because I was the newest officer
there, and the Fort Commandant was very much a
'Young Man's Commander', always one for giving
the juniors their chance. It all went splendidly till
we came to the end of the barrack rows, and, then,
just as we were about to turn back, the Legate
checked, and stood like a hound pointing into the
wind, an expression of alert interest on his face
that was beautiful to see. 'And down there?' he
demanded.

'Only the latrines, Sir,' said the Fort Commandant.

The Legate glanced round at him. 'Well? What are we waiting for?'

That was the first time I'd ever seen Centurion Titus Fulvius Lentullus, our Fort Commandant, look – not quite in command of the situation. He actually stuttered slightly. 'Sir – d-do I understand that you wish – '

And the Legate grinned at him: 'Didn't think I'd want to inspect the latrines, did you? They never do. That's why I always inspect 'em. A well-run camp or fort has well-kept latrines.'

And off he set.

Centurion Lentullus and my own Commander cast one anguished glance at each other. There was no time to send anyone ahead to make sure that all was well. We could only pray to our Gods and follow the Legate at a smart trot.

At the latrine doorway we were met by a burst of laughter from inside, then a quickly muttered warning, a gasp, and a long, horrified silence, as the men realized who and what was upon them.

Someone had been repainting the timbers and had left a paint-pot handy; Trooper Pertinax had made good use of it.

Nearly life-size on the blank white wall, outlined in a few masterly strokes, was the portrait of a very small Legate under a very large plumed helmet, his legs so bandy that they formed almost a complete circle under him!

Well he couldn't – Pertinax couldn't! – have expected any more than the rest of us that the

Legate would decide to inspect the latrines! I can
see his face now, and it went green; so did the faces
of the other men in there; two or three of them
beside Pertinax were my own troopers. I went over
in my mind the likely penalties for drawing a rude
portrait of one's Legate on a latrine wall – a portrait
seen by the Legate, at that – and they were fairly
savage. The silence seemed to drag out long and
thin.

The Legate broke in, in a voice like the crackling
of dry sticks. 'It seems you have an artist in your
midst.'

The Commandant seemed on the verge of
apoplexy. 'Sir – I can only assume – '

And then from somewhere, courage came to me,
the courage of absolute despair. And I heard my
own voice in the hideous silence: 'And one with a
remarkable gift for portraits of his fellows! But he
would have been wiser not to have painted one of
his Decurian!'

I stepped out in front of the rest, to let the Legate
get a good view of me, bow legs and all. I made as
though I was going to hit Pertinax across the face,
but I didn't have to. The Commander caught on
quickly: 'Decurian Calpurnius, this matter will be
dealt with properly at a more fitting time.'

Pertinax caught on quickly, too, and stared at his
feet and scuffled. The moment before, he'd been
looking like a man facing death.

The Legate stood and looked from me to the

drawing on the wall and back again. 'The helmet looks somewhat – elaborate, for a troop leader.'

I said, 'Parade helmet, Sir – cavalry manoeuvres!'

And I looked him straight in the eye; and he looked straight back and never blinked, though I saw the laughter twitch once at the corner of his mouth. He was a great man.

'Ah yes,' he said, 'the cavalry manoeuvres. Tomorrow afternoon, I understand. I look forward to witnessing them.'

And he went on with the inspection.

Very late that night, when I was checking over my equipment for next day, my Second came to my quarters, and when I bade him come in, he still hovered, just inside the doorway.

I looked up from the buckle I was testing. 'Well? What is it, Number Two?'

He saluted and came in, then, rather stiffly, and set something down on the table: something that gleamed fish-scale colour in the lamplight. 'I came to bring you this, Sir.'

I picked it up. 'My bracelet! How in the world did you come by it?'

'The lads thought you might like it back before tomorrow,' he said.

He meant 'before the Fire-ride' of course. I was still young to soldiering, and I had not yet ceased to be surprised at how much troops always know about their officers. I said, 'But in the Name of Light, how did they get hold of it?'

'I would not ask, Sir,' he said, staring straight in front of him.

'You mean they – they – '

'They went to a deal of trouble to get it, Sir.'

I looked at the battered bracelet, and just for the moment I couldn't speak. Then I held it out to my Second. 'I am very sure they did. But I cannot take it until it has been properly redeemed. Number Two, will you ask them now to take as much trouble to get it back to Decurian Florianus – before he misses it, if possible. And thank them for me – thank them *very much* for me, Number Two.'

He looked at me for a moment. Then he took the bracelet: 'I'll tell them, Sir.' And the 'Sir' had none of that shade too much respect. He saluted, and swung on his heel, and marched out.

From the rampart, the trumpet sounded for the Third Watch. It was already the day of the cavalry manoeuvres.

All the town, as well as the fort, turned out to watch, that afternoon, thronging the sloping turf banks of the parade-ground that Three Headed Hill looks down on. And the sellers of honeycakes and cheap wine were doing a roaring trade. It was a fine day, too, the sunshine just silvered by a faint haze, and just enough wind to stir the blue and yellow plumes of the parade helmets and the long silken dragon-body of the cavalry standard. And the horses seemed to catch the general excitement, tossing their heads and dancing a little as they waited. I remember the eager feel of Ajax gathering himself under me, the way he arched his neck and ruckled softly down his nose, the strange pungent smell of the herbs with which his hide had been treated against the Fire-ride.

Then the trumpets sounded, and troop after troop, we moved off, First Troop, Second, Third. . . . It was our turn. I heeled Ajax into a canter, the rest behind me, and we were off, Ajax's nose the regulation two-and-a-half spears' lengths from the tail of Number Six Troop's rear horse; out through the Dexter Gate and on to the parade ground, dividing, troop by troop, left and right as we went, until the whole Cohort was drawn up in two long lines facing each other across the width of the open space.

The trumpets yauped again, and again the horses broke from a stand into a canter. Sweeping in towards each other, to meet and pass, each horse and rider through the narrow gap between his opposite numbers on either side; then wheel about to face each other again. The show had begun.

Troop by troop, we wheeled and turned, weaving intricate patterns of ourselves at full gallop. The wind of our going, flowing into the open-mouthed silver head of the Cohort dragon, filled the long silken tube of its body, so that it whipped out like a writhing crimson flame behind the galloping standard bearer, and the flame was echoed by the flickering many-coloured troop-pennants following behind. And the lift and laughter of the heart, that must not for a moment break one's concentration, rose in each of us. And all the world was full of the beat of hooves, and the wind in our faces, and the yelp of the trumpets keeping the time and signalling the changes of formation.

We kept the Fire-ride till last of all. The three banks of brushwood were laid and lit, and blazed up red in the thin sunlight, bending over where the breeze caught the tips of the flames. We remounted our blindfolded horses, and I rode out in front of the troop, and wheeled about to look at them. We had taken off our cloaks and the great masked and plumed parade helmets – the less we had about us that could catch fire, the better – and so all the faces that looked back at me were bare. Pertinax was there on the left of the line; he caught my eye and grinned. All along the line, I looked, and, suddenly, I knew that the thing had happened. Number Seven Troop was mine! And I was theirs!

'If you can earn their respect and their trust, they'll follow you through fire and flood,' the Cohort Commander had said. Well, there wasn't any flood. . . .

'Ready, Sir,' my Second said.

'Ready, Number Two!'

I wheeled Ajax, and jabbed my heel into his flank and raised the high Dacian yell as he sprang forward. Behind me I heard the drum of hooves, and the yell taken up by the rest of the troop.

It is a strange and wonderful thing that a horse will charge blindly into the dark if he knows and trusts his rider and the hand on the guiding rein.

Ours neither checked nor swerved, but charged down straight and true upon the first of the fire-hedges. The crowd began to roar. I steadied Ajax at the last moment, felt the willing strength of his haunches gather under me. I had my face driven down into his mane. The smell of the herbs on his hide was in my throat, along with the smell of his sweat and the acrid reek of the fire. There was a moment of blasting heat, and then we were through, and racing down upon the second wall of flame. Time to snatch one gulp of clean air before the heat and the choking smoke and the raw, red blast of heat engulfed us a second time. Then that too was behind us; and ahead of us the last and broadest fire-hedge of all. The roar of the crowd rose like a stormy sea, and above it, muffled in our horses' manes, we raised the wild, savage triumph of the Dacian victory yell. For a moment all the world was smoke and flame and a searing furnace-blast of heat; and then for the third time we were through and sweeping on. We charged at a thunder-ing gallop right up to the edge of the dais of piled turfs where the Legate sat; and brought the horses up all standing.

The Legate sat unmoving, and waited, until we had the horses quieted and in perfect line before him; and then nodded to me. 'That was worth seeing. Your troop does you credit, Decurian.'

We tossed up our swords to him as we rode off, that great little man with the bow legs.

And we were well pleased with ourselves.

There's not much more to tell, really. . . . Trooper Pertinax went up before the Commander next day, and got another spell of Confined to Barracks for drawing an unflattering portrait of his Troop Leader on the latrine wall. And I redeemed the family bracelet when I got my next month's pay, and never played dice with Florianus again.

But it was when the Fire-ride was just over, that I suddenly realized I hadn't missed it – the bracelet – because I had gained something else that gave me all the confidence I needed. . . .

I've been lucky in the troops and later the cohorts, that I've led in my time; but I've never loved any of them quite as I came to love Number Seven Troop of the Dacian Horse.

4

Traprain Law AD 196

I speak to you now; I, Struan, brother to Sualtam that is a Clan Chieftain of the Votadini, and foster son to Fergal the Bronzesmith who lives and has his smithy where the old chariot road comes in from the South to the foot of Traprain Law.

When I was a child, I was small and weakly, so that they did not think I had it in me to make a warrior. And it was so that my father the Chieftain gave me to Fergal instead of to one of his Spear-Companions according to the usual custom, in the hope that at least I might have it in me to make a craftsman. But as I grew older, I grew strong – small, still, but tough, like a heather root – and so I became a warrior after all.

Fergal was glad for me; but for himself, he grieved, I think, because after Gault, my foster brother, died of the end-of-winter fever, he had no son to follow him in his trade. And I, I was glad to have my place among the warriors; but whenever I was Traprain way, I went back to the house-place beside the old chariot road, as a son going home.

Traprain Law. . . . Long before the Romans came, the King of the Votadini had his turf-banked stronghold and his timber halls on the crest of the hill. And little by little the swordsmiths and the horsedealers, the workers in gold and enamels, and the weavers of bright chequered cloth, the chariot builders and the makers of songs, all the people who gather to a King's Court, built their living places on the slopes below. I have seen other towns and cities in the South, where men have said: 'Now we will build a Basilica or a triumphal arch with a statue of an Emperor on top of it – and then we shall be truly Roman.' Traprain was never like that. Always it has been British; turf-roofed, stone and wattle walled, with crooked and winding ways that snake about the hillside, and stone hearths where the wandering harpers make their songs in the evening. And never a triumphal arch in sight, nor a statue of an Emperor sitting on a too-fat horse. But for the most part, there has been friendship between the Votadini and the Romans. We have bought and sold from each other, and with the buying and selling, and the making for the Roman market, Traprain has grown to be a town.

In my eighteenth summer (it was the year Clodius Albinus the Governor of Britain took so many troops overseas to make himself Emperor), I followed Sualtam who was by then Chieftain in our father's place to the great yearly Gathering at Traprain. That is when all the Clan Chieftains and the great men of the Tribe came together in Council to settle disputes and make and remake laws, to speak, each for their own clan, and to listen to the voice of the King.

The Council was held in the forecourt of the King's House, the King himself sitting on a pile of black bulls' hides before the doorway of his Hall, and beside him on a pile, just one hide lower, the Government Inspector in his clean white tunic and violet-bordered mantle, to see that the laws of Rome as well as the laws of the Votadini were served. And we young braves of the Chieftain's following sat on our haunches behind our Spear-Lords, and passed the time as best we might. And along the sunlit side of the Hall, the troopers of Dacian Cavalry who formed the Inspector's escort kicked their heels, as bored as we.

But when the day's Council was over, then we were free, to feast in the King's Hall if we chose, or go about our own affairs.

I took the short cut down through the Potters' quarter – Traprain makes much pottery (poor stuff, but the Legions don't call for fine red Samian ware to drink their wine out of), and came to my foster-father's doorway.

Inside was the glow of the forge fire, and there I saw my foster-father, naked save for his leather apron, his shoulders hunched and strong as he bent over the piece of metal that he was working up on the anvil. The metal glowed red, and so did his hair that was close-curled as a ram's fleece; the hair on the outsides of his arms was golden, tinged with the same red. Above the ding of hammer on anvil and the hoarse roar of the fire which he had just blown up, he did not hear me come, and I stood in the doorway and called.

'Fergal, my foster-father!'

He looked up, then; and flung down his hammer, wiping the back of a hand across his sweaty face, and came striding to meet me. 'Struan! Fosterling! Hi Mi! It is as good as ten hot suppers to see you again!'

'And you! Oh, it is good to be back!' We were hugging like a couple of bearcubs, and beating each other about the shoulders. 'Is there any supper? Where is Murna?'

'Easy! Easy!' Fergal said. 'One question at a time! There is supper – your favourite, boar meat baked with honey; and Murna has gone to the market for some wine. We knew that you would be home before the last sunlight left the doorsill.'

It was a fine reunion, and we had scarcely done beating each other on the shoulders when the doorway darkened, and I looked round, thinking to see Murna my foster-sister with the wine; I saw instead a trooper of the Inspector's escort, standing there with the last sunlight jinking on the bronze comb of his helmet.

'This is the forge of Fergal the Bronzesmith?' he said.

'It is so. And I am Fergal. What would you have of me?'

The man pulled off a bracelet that he wore high under the sleeve of his leather tunic. 'I am told that you are as skilled with silver as with bronze. Can you set this to rights for me?'

Fergal took it from him and looked at it, turning it to the light. 'Ayee!' he drew in his breath between his teeth. 'That is a dunt! A sword cut, I would be thinking?'

'Aye!' The man nodded, 'And would have laid my arm bare to the bone if this had not turned the blade.'

I had come up to look also. The bracelet was scratched and scarred by many marks beside the sword dint, but I could still see quite clearly the device engraved on it; it was a Capricorn, half goat, half fish, and the thing caught my interest. 'It is a Legionary bracelet, is it not, then? I have seen others of the kind before, but not quite the same – it looks old – and as though it will have seen hard service.'

'*Struan!*' said my foster-father below his breath. He was shamed by my ill manners, for among the Tribes it is ill done to ask questions of a stranger, at least until he has eaten and drunk beneath one's roof; and though I had not in truth asked, the question was there.

But the man looked round at me with one eyebrow cocked in a way that I was to come to know. He was not so much older than I; maybe two or three and twenty, with a quick face, and the bluest eyes that I have ever seen in any man. 'Notice things, don't you?' he said. 'Yes, it is old, and it

has seen hard service. It belonged to the first of our family to follow the Eagles.'

And at that moment, Murna arrived back from the market.

She was calling before she was in from the road. 'Struan! Struan!' And then she checked in the doorway at sight of the stranger.

I put my arms round her, wine jug and all, and hugged her close and close. No blood-sister could have been nearer to me than she was. And she laughed, and tried to push me away. 'Oh, be careful! Let you be careful of the wine!'

My foster-father had turned his back on us and was attending to his customer. 'I can beat this out for you cold; it will take but a short time – if you will come back later this evening, I will have it ready for you.' And then it seemed that an idea came to him out of the rejoicing that was in the air. 'Or stay, since you are come in a happy hour when my foster-son returns to us for a while, bide and drink a cup of wine while I set all to rights.'

The soldier smiled. 'It is a kindly offer, and most gladly I accept it.'

So Murna went to fetch out from the inner room the cup of green Roman glass that was always kept for honoured guests; and filled it with wine for the soldier. And I saw how all the time his eyes followed her. But I think that, at that time, he was one whose eyes follow any girl who is not as ugly as the Furies, and Murna – well, it is hard to tell with one's own kin – she was not ugly; she had a kind, quiet face that lit up when she was happy.

My foster-father had put aside whatever was on the anvil, and begun work already on the dinted bracelet; and Murna brought the cup to the soldier. 'Drink, stranger, and be welcome.'

And the soldier took it gravely from between her two hands. It seemed he knew his manners, and the manners of Tribes. 'Good fortune on the house, and on the woman of the house!' And then he smiled: 'And my name is Lucian.'

Murna repeated it after him, 'Lucian', very quietly and smiled also.

Then she filled one of the household cups of black pottery for me, and we sat on the bench against the wall, drinking and talking, while she went about her task of making ready the supper, and Fergal worked on at the dinted silver bracelet.

And when the repair was finished, Lucian paid for it, and sprang the thing back on to his arm, and went his way.

That was the first time I ever saw Lucianus Calpurnius, who was to change all my life for me. But on the last night of the Gathering, I met him again.

The day had been mostly filled with a dispute between two Clans as to the borders of their hunting runs – dry and dusty stuff, old men's talk drawn from the memories of their grandfathers – and he was making for one of the wine booths in the fairground that always sprang up below Traprain at Gathering time. I took him instead to the House of

Talore, where you can get good beer and barley fire-drink in place of the sour wine they sell in the fairground.

Besides, if you must be having the truth, I was hoping that somebody I knew might be there, for I was proud to be seen with Lucian. So tall, he seemed to me, and noonday splendid. And he had not laughed at me for my small size and midnight colour, saying that my true mother must have been one of the Little Dark People, as my brother and the men of our Clan sometimes did, maybe not knowing how the jest galled me. . . .

The House of Talore was a favourite gathering place for merchant folk, and, even as we ducked through the low doorway into the firelit gloom and the peat reek hanging low under the thatch, I heard a voice I knew well. Flann the Far-Wanderer, who traded in pottery with the far North, and had even been to the Islands of Thule at the world's end, was as full of traveller's tales as an egg is full of meat.

'And I tell you, it is only the bravest of the brave, who may reach to those islands,' he was saying. 'For beside the storms and the wild wastes of waters, they are hedged about with walls of freezing fog through which one must sail for days on end. And out of the fog the great tusked sea-beasts rise up to attack any ship that comes that way. And the people of those islands are squat as toads, and slit-eyed, and yellow, and have strange powers to make the hair rise on the back of your neck – '

'But they are knowing a good pot when they see one,' somebody put in, and there was a general laugh.

'And why would they not be knowing a good pot when they see one?' Flann said. 'But I see that I am wasting my time talking to you of things that are beyond your understanding.'

We bought heather beer, a jug between us, and settled down in a corner to talk. And so, friendli-wise, we both learned something that evening of each other and each other's worlds.

And all the while, behind me – for he must have decided that he was not wasting his time after all – I could hear Flann the Far-Wanderer, still in full spate. . . . 'And on those islands there are great jets of boiling water, taller than the topmost branch of the tenth tree, if ten tall trees were set one upon another. And there are mountains plumed with fire. . . .'

But I was more interested in what Lucian was saying.

'It's not such a bad life – oh I'm not talking about the Legions, of course, not nowadays, but the Auxiliaries. And the Dacian Horse are the best of them. If you're a Chief's son, you'd like enough get command of a troop before long, and a Cohort by and by. And there's always the chance of seeing other lands – like our friend yonder. Think about it, Struan.'

'I will be thinking about it,' I said, staring into

the honey-brown depths of my beer. And indeed I was already thinking – hard!

And, then, someone else came through the low doorway, and a kind of breath of stillness ran through the crowded houseplace. Even Flann, finding that nobody was listening to him, let his story fall away. And everyone looked towards the newcomer. But indeed we were the newcomers, not she. Not the small dark-haired woman with the necklace of dried seedpods and berries and blue jay's feathers strung about her neck! Long, long before the Romans marched north, long, long before we, the Votadini, came to Traprain Law, the Little Dark Ones were the people of this land. Now, they live among the high moors and the waste places, and we see little of them. But sometimes they come down to sell beaver and wildcat skins, to beg for the scraps that we do not want, and steal whatever they can lay their hands on. And sometimes at the great feasts, or at the Gathering, one bolder than the rest – generally a woman – will come to our drinking houses, and make a little of the simpler kind of magic for the customers there, in return for a belly full of food and drink and perhaps an old cloak or a chipped pot. Some people laugh at them for mere tricksters, but there are few that laugh twice.

The woman stood in the doorway, with the dusk spread behind her and the fingers of the firelight just brushing her bare feet, and looked round at us. And when she spoke, her voice was dark also, with a kind of bloom on it, like the bloom on a wild sloe. 'Peace and plenty be upon the house and all within the house. Would my Lords see a small magic?'

The silence in the ale-shop broke up, as Talore himself bade her enter, and others added their voices to his.

'Aye, come in and work your magic.'

'Can you conjure up a smoke-man from the fire?'

'Cast us a spell to make the beer stronger, Old Mother.'

And there was a scraping of stools and benches on the earthen floor as men turned themselves round to the hearth. And the woman came in and took her stand by the fire, seeming strangely far off from it all.

'So,' she said, when something of the quiet had come back again. 'It shall be as my Lords command. Let one of my Lords give me a thing to hold – a small thing for a small magic.' Her gaze moved over us all, not hurrying, nor yet lingering, till it rested upon Flann. 'You, Far-Wanderer, let you lend me the blue ring from your hand.'

Flann pulled off the ring and gave it to her. 'Take good care of it, then, it is a rare stone of much value.'

I saw it clearly, lying on the woman's narrow brown palm; a common ring of copper wire with a blue glass bead on it. There were nine or ten of us there, and we all crowded in to look.

'Aye,' she said, 'look closely, look, and see – '

Her voice took on a soft crooning note like a wood pigeon's on a hot day, that makes one sleepy just to hear it. 'And see – and see. . . .'

I mind it had been a very still night until that moment, but a little stray sighing of wind seemed to rise suddenly out of nowhere, setting the peat-smoke swirling across our eyes, then sank away. ' – and see – and see – ' said the crooning voice. 'Look closely, closely, now it begins, now the seed springs and the tree is growing. Do you see – and see – and see. . . .'

At first, there was just the ring, and a fleck of blue light from the fire in the heart of the glass bead. Then the light began to spread until her palm was full of it, brimming as a cup brims with wine. And out of the heart of the blue radiance, there began to grow a little tree. First the winter twig, and then the buds, swelling and opening, leaf after leaf. Seven leaves I counted; and on the topmost twig there perched a small bird – it could have been a goldfinch – and in its beak was the ring.

For maybe the space of seven heartbeats it remained, clear for us all to see; it was perfect, the most perfect thing that I have ever seen. Every vein in every leaf, every feather of the bird's raised crest singing with a kind of cool blue marsh-light that was brighter than all the hearth fires of Traprain Law. And then the woman slapped her free hand down over it; and when she raised her hand again, there was only the glass and copper ring lying in her thin brown palm.

We looked round at each other, blinking a little as though waking from sleep. Someone spread his fingers in the sign against evil. Someone called loudly for more beer. Someone tossed her a barley cake from the dish that he and his friends had been sharing. Lucian said: 'Little Mother, that was a magic worth the watching.'

Flann snorted. 'Pugh! The merest trick! Why, in the Islands of the North, I have seen the dwarf wizards cast a spell upon two men, so that they got up from sharing the same food bowl, and fought to the death with long knives. That was a *real* magic.'

The woman smiled, very faintly. 'As my Lord says, they make magic in the North. Take your ring again. Is it unharmed? Just as it was when you gave it to me?'

Flann glanced at it as he pushed it back on to his finger. 'Aye, what should – '

'Look again,' the woman said. 'Look well, and make sure – and very sure. . . .'

And Flann spread his fingers and looked again at the ring. 'No,' he said slowly after a moment. 'It seems – changed.'

'How, changed?' Again, the woman's voice had taken on the wood pigeon note; again, the little wind eddied the peat-smoke across our eyes. 'Look again, and look well – and well – and well!'

And Flann looked and looked, as though he was caught in some kind of dream. And against all nature, I'll swear that the spark of light in the heart of that bit of blue glass was purplish red. A red star, a red eye. Then he looked up, slowly. His eyes were strange, cloudy, and with the same red spark at the back of them. He stared round at us all, his head out-thrust and low between his shoulders. And then he went fighting mad!

It was not that he came at any particular one of us; he gave a strange, low, snarling cry, and whipped his knife from his belt, and went for us all together, like a wild beast striking at random against a ring of hunters.

Lucian grappled with him and got a grip on the wrist of his dagger hand, shouting: 'Drop it! Drop it, you madman!' They strained together a few moments, while the rest of us closed in. The knife went clattering, and somebody kicked it out through the open doorway. But he seemed to have the strength of ten men even when he was disarmed. He got home a blow to Lucian's face, and the heavy glass ring sliced his cheek to the bone. Most of us had a mark of some sort by the time we pulled him down. I got him by the ears and cracked his head on the hearth-stone a couple of times. It seemed the best thing to be doing.

When he was quiet at last, and we looked round for the Little Dark Woman, she was gone.

In a while, Flann began to moan and gurgle and show signs of coming back into himself, so Talore heaved half a pail of water over him to help him find the way. When he opened his eyes, the red was quite gone from them; and he tried to sit up, groaning, 'Och, my *head!* – what happened?'

'You went mad and tried to kill us all, that's what happened,' Talore said.

And Lucian added: 'It seems it is not only in the Islands of the North that they make real magic.'

He had pulled off his neckerchief, and was dabbing at the cut on his cheek, spreading the blood about, without doing any great good.

'You cannot be going back to your fellows in that state,' I said. 'Best that you come home with me; and let Murna tend it for you.'

I took him back to my foster-father's house, and through into the houseplace behind the forge. Murna was bending over the evening stew, and she cried out at the sight of Lucian's face, and made him sit on a low stool beside the hearth while she warmed some water. And while I stood by to hold the lamp, she bathed and salved the cut.

I mind that was the first time, watching her, I noticed that her hands and her voice were both beautiful.

'Bend your head that way; there, now I can see. . . . Oh, it was a wicked thing to do!'

'He did not know what he was doing.'

'I did not mean Flann – the Woman. It was a wicked thing to do.'

Lucian said, consideringly: 'I suppose with magic, as with any craft, any skill, it must be hard when men who do not have the wit to understand, belittle the thing you make. It must be hard always to use the small skill, to make a little tree grow out of nothing, to amuse people whom you scorn in your heart, when you know that you have within you the power to make – the other thing.'

Fergal, who had come in from the forge, said: 'That does not sound like hardheaded Rome.'

'As to that,' Lucian turned his head between Murna's hands, 'my father was more than half British, and my grandmother was of the Votadini.'

He caught his breath, and Murna said quickly: 'Oh, did I hurt you? I will try to be gentle.'

'You are very gentle,' Lucian said. 'If ever I am wounded, it is you that I shall come to, to make me well again, Murna.'

'I will remember. Turn your face further to the light.'

In the end, he stayed to eat with us. And after, my foster-father went out again to the forge, for he was at work on a set of shield-mountings that must be finished that night. I went to work the goatskin bellows for him in case he should need the fire, though, at this final stage, I knew that for the most part he would be working the bronze cold – bronze, given to the fire too often, becomes brittle under the hammer. And Lucian, on his way out to go back to his troop, checked to watch.

The shield-boss lay on the anvil, still stained violet and greyish-black in places from the fire. The raised design of curve and counter-curve that folded in upon each other like a still half-opened bracken frond, carried one's eye round the thing, satisfying the sight in the same way that holding something smooth and round satisfies the palm of one's hand.

Fergal picked it up and turned with it to the work bench, and began to give it the final working-over. Lucian, bending close to watch, said: 'This is most beautiful. This curve like the arch of a stallion's neck – and here – and here again. . . . It must be good to make such a thing as this. To know the dream of it in one's mind and in one's heart, and see the thing one knows growing under one's hands.'

'It is good,' my foster-father said. 'And now it is finished, save for the burnishing before it goes to the shieldmaker in the morning. The shield rim is in the corner yonder, let you bring it to me.' And when Lucian did, as he bade him: 'Now hold it – so.' And I think without either of them noticing what they did, they began to work together.

'Now turn it a little – this way. Hold steady.'

And watching them, it came to me suddenly that they looked in some way as though they fitted, as though they had worked together for years.

After a while, Fergal, my foster-father, said: 'Fate plays strange tricks; you, who are a soldier, have craftsman's hands. Did you know that? While Struan here, who was once to have been a bronze-smith, has the hands for a sword.' And then he laughed: 'If ever you think to change your craft, come to me, and I will teach you mine.'

When he left, I went with him to the door, and he flung an arm across my shoulders in parting: 'Think about joining the Eagles. We might serve together, one day.'

I did think about it. Most of that night, I thought, and – I am still not sure why, except that I had found a soldier to call friend, which, I suppose, has been reason enough for many a one before my time, and since – when my brother and his spear-companions rode home, I rode on south, alone. Four days south, to Corstopitum, the big depot town behind the Wall; I told the Duty Centurion at the fort that I had come to be a soldier.

Oh, they took me readily enough! They had a sore need of men that year, and before I was through my training, word came that Clodius Albinus had been defeated and slain, and most of his troops with him. And, as had happened more than once before, the Tribes seized their chance to revolt. From the old Northern Wall that followed Agricola's line of forts, right down to Eburacum, the world went up in flames.

I heard once that the Dacian Cavalry, along with other forces, had been sent up to hold back the Tribes that were pouring down from Outland Caledonia. I was sent off, still half-trained, to join what was left of the garrison at Eburacum.

And then the Emperor Severus sent reinforcements, under a new Governor, and, after a while, the Red Time passed, and orders came again. And so, more than two years since my last coming, I went home to my foster-father's house. The Votadini had been split between those who held by Rome and those who followed the Tribes. And all Traprain Law bore the scars of fire and fighting.

They had begun to rebuild by the time I came back. Timber and thatch is easily built up again; it would take longer to fill the empty places that dead men had left behind them, and for the look of famine to fade from the faces of the living.

But already trade was returning to the town; and on the third day of my leave, my foster-father was busy in the forge, with myself again working the bellows for him, when someone came in from the Chariot Way.

He wore the travel-stained wreck of an old military tunic; he looked old and gaunt, and he leaned heavily on a staff. And it must have been three heartbeats of time before I knew him.

'Lucian!', 'Struan!', we cried in the same instant. And then he said, looking at my own tunic: 'You took my advice, I see.'

He hobbled forward, and next moment I had my arm round him. 'Here now, sit down on the bench. What is amiss with your leg?'

'A Pictish arrow through my knee,' he said, and stuck it out stiff before him as he sat down. 'It's quite an old wound, but I've – walked rather too far on it.'

Fergal came to stand over him. There was an odd look on his face, I mind, a kind of waiting look. He said, 'And what brings you walking *this* way, Lucian of the Dacian Horse?'

Lucian looked up at him. 'Do you remember once bidding me come to you if ever I thought to change my craft?'

'I do,' Fergal said, looking back.

'You laughed; we all laughed. But – did you mean it?'

'Assuredly I meant it.'

Lucian's mouth twisted into something like his old quick smile – but not very like! 'I am glad, because the Eagles have no more use for me, and these past two years have left me no one else to go to.' His head tipped back against the wall: 'I am so tired.'

And then Murna came through the inner doorway. She must have heard what passed in the smithy, and known who was there, but maybe she had needed those few breaths of time. . . . Also she had waited to fill a cup with milk. And I mind that I noticed, even in that moment, that it was not the green glass cup, but a black pottery bowl such as she would have brought *me*. And I knew that Lucian was no longer a guest in the house.

'Also you promised that if ever you were wounded, you would come to me to be made well again,' she said.

Aye well, it's all a long time ago. They called the second son Struan after me, so I've always taken an interest in him. He's serving with the Sixth British Cohort on the Danube, now.

I have wondered, sometimes, if the Little Dark Woman knew just how great a magic she made in the House of Talore that night. For if Flann the Far-Wanderer had not laid Lucian's cheek open so that I brought him home to our house for Murna's tending, so much that happened afterwards might never have happened at all.

My life was already on the change, but the Little Dark Woman changed Lucian's life, and the life of Murna my foster-sister, who was not even there. And Struan, my namesake, would never have been born at all.

And I'm thinking that was as great a magic as any spell that was ever woven by the dwarf wizards in the Islands of the North.

5
Frontier Post AD 280

Most families have their handed-down treasures, I
suppose. With us, it's a battered old Legionary
bracelet: a silver 'Distinguished Conduct' bracelet,
embossed with the Capricorn badge of the Second
Augustan. The story goes that it belonged to the
first of the family to follow the Eagles, and that he
earned it on one of Agricola's Caledonian campaigns. But that's two hundred years ago, and a
story can gather a bit of moss in two hundred years.
But sometimes when I'm giving it a rub up along
with the rest of my tack, I wonder what he'd have
thought of us, nowadays, the Lucius who first
owned that bracelet, whether he'd have recognized
us as his army at all. There's been a good many
changes since he took his Wooden Foil! . . . *Us*,
for instance; we didn't exist in his day, nor for a
long time afterwards.

In the Official Army Lists we're entered as Ex-
ploratores, but for ordinary daily use, we answer to
the name of Frontier Scouts. And among ourselves
– and among the Tribes – we're the Frontier
Wolves, for fairly obvious reasons. We're mostly
native born, or a mixture of Roman and Tribesman
like me; and no self-respecting Legionary would be

seen dead in our company. (*We* don't feel all that brotherly towards the Legionaries, come to that.) But they'd be in a sore way without us. We're the Eyes and Ears of the Frontier, and when need be, the Hunters and the Teeth-in-the-dark.

When I was young, so young that I hadn't yet got my wolfskin cloak – oh yes, I forgot to say that one of our traditions is that we wear wolfskin cloaks instead of the thick grey woollen ones that are army issue, and each man has to kill his own wolf to get it – yes, well, when I was as young as that, I served a couple of years at Credigone, right up at the eastern end of what used to be the old Northern Wall. The fort was abandoned years ago; but in those days, when Votadini territory ran for a while almost to the mouths of the Highland glens, we used to patrol right up as far as the Tava.

We used to be out ten, twelve days at a time, sleeping in our cloaks by our picketed ponies at night, and all day long, the hills swimming in the August heat or the man next ahead of you half lost in rain-mist or driving snow. No sound on the high moors but the wind and the curlews crying, and the brushing of our horses' legs through the heather. Patrols and patrols and patrols. . . .

There was one in particular, in my second autumn, that I'll not be forgetting in a hurry.

We were just about at our furthest point from base, heading down the curve of a long glen that opens into the Tava levels. The ten of us were riding well strung out, keeping to the higher ground but firmly below the skyline. 'Never get sky-lined' is one of the first lessons you learn, at our game – I've said that that was all Votadini territory, and officially it was, but we were near to the Pictish border, and only a fool goes *looking* for trouble. And just as we rounded the hill flank into sight of the river, up starts something out of the brown heather under the very nose of the Decurian's horse. Not a Pict, but one of the Little Dark Folk who were here before the painted Picts and the Lowland Tribes alike. We're mostly on pretty good terms with them; we'll share our food and the warmth of a campfire with them, which the Tribes will never do, and give them a trifle of protection from time to time. And in return, they don't steal our horses, and they bring us the occasional bit of news.

Fiends and Furies! But you should have heard the Decurian curse! Soft but splendid, as you might say, while he got his startled horse back under control. When it had ceased its squealing and trampling, he turned his attention to the cause. 'Curithir! Cross-eyed, lop-eared son of a witless mother! Is it that you think you are a blackcock to come starting up under a horse's nose like that?'

The small man stood and looked up at him, sideways a little, under his brows, in the way of his kind. 'I have a thing to show My Lord.'

'Show then,' Decurian Rufus said.

The Little Dark One drew a long knife – a kind

of dirk, but of a pattern I had not seen before, from under his deerskin mantle, and held it out: 'I show!'

Rufus caught his breath, and bent down quickly to take the thing. 'I have seen the like of this in the South before ever I ran with the wolf-pack. It is a Saxon Long-knife.'

'I did well to bring it to My Lord?'

'You did well. How did you come by it?'

'I found it on a man that I killed. I thought it was like no knife that I had seen before.'

'Where did you kill him, this man?'

'Across the river,' Curithir said, jerking his chin northward, 'towards the High King's Hall. Does My Lord wish to see for himself?'

Decurian Rufus stuck the knife in his belt. 'Yes, and as soon as may be. Lucius, you'll come with me. Bericus, take over while I'm away – get back up the glen a bit, and wait for me!'

We left our horses with the rest of the troop, and headed for Tavaside on foot, forded the river at the first shallows, and followed down the further side, striking inland after a while, and making good use of every scrap of cover. Suddenly Curithir dived into a bramble thicket and went to work on a tangle of dead bracken and thorn branches, like a dog digging up a bone.

The man he uncovered with a satisfied grunt lay face down; it was growing dusk, but there was still light enough to see the dark stain between his shoulder blades where the spear had gone in.

'Roll him over,' the Decurian said.

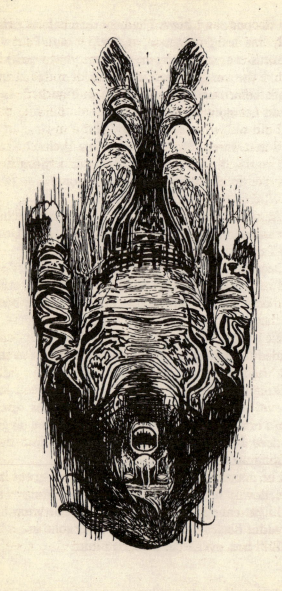

I stooped, and heaved him on to his back. His body had had time to stiffen, and he came over all in one like a wooden figure. He was yellow-haired, with pale eyes. He wore the kind of rough, dark clothes that might have come from anywhere and would not show up against an autumn hillside, but on both his wrists were heavy gold arm-rings of a kind that were strange to me. And still clutched in one hand was a green hazel branch scarcely touched with yellow. It must have been quite a task to find one still so green at that time of year.

'So-o, a herald,' the Decurian said. 'And Saxon, sure enough. Curithir, why did you kill him?'

'Because of another thing I saw.'

'And what thing was that?'

But Curithir was telling his story in his own way. 'A thing! And I followed him, and he went toward the Hall of Bruide the High King, with a herald's green branch in his hand, and in secret; and it came into my heart that it was maybe better he did not reach the High King.'

'And so you made sure.'

'And so I made sure, and came to tell you.' Curithir showed his teeth like a dog.

'How did you know where to find me?' Decurian Rufus was not one to let loose ends lying.

Curithir raised one finger in the air and blew on it delicately. 'Not a beetle crawls on a blade of grass, that the Little Dark People do not know.'

'Mithras! Why do we trouble to patrol these hills at all?' said the Decurian, and returned to his original question: 'What is this other thing that you saw?'

This time Curithir was ready to answer. 'A ship – two ships. Not Roman!'

'*Where?*'

'Come; I show.'

We covered the dead man over again, quickly but carefully, and set off on the heels of our little savage. It was the first time I'd been up into Pictish country, though it wasn't the last. And I still sweat cold when I think of that long stalk down Tavaside in the windy autumn dusk! It was well into the night when we came at last over the crest of a low ridge of hazel woods; and Curithir checked and reached back a warning hand to the Decurian who passed the silent warning on to me. We froze for a few moments, then dropped on to all-fours and oozed forward again, bellies to the ground. The moon, swimming out from the clouds, showed us a narrow inlet, well shielded from the open river – hazel and alder scrub growing right down to a pebbly shore, and on the shore, pulled up clear of the tide-line, the dark shapes of two long slim warboats, high at stem and stern. Figures moved on the beach, and someone spoke in a guttural tongue, and there was a breath of laughter, and then all was quiet again save for the wind hushing through the hazel scrub.

We all knew of the sea-raiders in the south, and the great forts that were being built against their attacks, along what was already beginning to be called the Saxon Shore; so there was no need to wonder what it was that we were looking at, down there.

The Decurian whispered: 'Get back a bit.'

And we backed on our tracks. You don't last long as a Frontier Wolf if you can't learn to move quickly and quietly in the wilderness, backwards as well as forwards, and Rufus and I could move almost as silently as Curithir himself. Not a dry grass stalk rustled, not a leaf stirred except in the wind as we melted back over the brow of the ridge. And in a small sheltered hollow on the far side, we checked again, and spoke together, quickly and at half-breath.

'So the Sea Wolves are creeping north,' I said.

'Aye, seeking to join spears with the Picts – or the Picts with the Sea Wolves. Against us, either way,' Decurian Rufus said. 'And the question is, how long will they wait, down there, for their herald to return with the High King's answer – or his summons – or whatever it is they wait for.'

Curithir spoke for the first time. 'For all that they can know, the High King may be sick or on the hunting trail. Many things may delay a herald. It is in my mind that they will wait at least a night and a day, and then another night, before they do any other thing. And in that time they will not break cover, lest news of their coming should spread south of the river and reach the ears of the Red Crests.'

('Red Crests' is the name the Little Dark Folk give to all the Roman army.)

'If you are right, that should give us time enough,' the Decurian said, 'and we must just pray to all the Gods there be that the Painted People do not find them for themselves, meanwhile. Lucius, get back to the rest, quick as you can make it. Report to Bericus and give him my orders to send a man back to Credigone for reinforcements – all they can spare, I doubt it will be more than a couple of troops – and bring the rest of the patrol up to the fording place. Curithir shall be waiting there to bring them on to me here. For yourself, pick up your own horse and get down to Inveresk. Take this ring of mine to the Commander of the fort to vouch for you – and request a couple of scouting galleys to cut off any retreat from the seaward side. Understood?'

I said, 'And, you, Sir?'

'I stay here to keep an eye on the quarry. *Understood?*'

'Understood, Sir,' I said.

'Away with you, then, and good luck!'

I needed it! If the outward stalk was bad, the return was worse. Gods! I'd not do it again for half a year's pay! But I got back to the waiting patrol at last, and passed on the Decurian's orders. I picked up my own horse, and, with the moon still high in the ragged sky, set off for the naval station at Inveresk.

I'd the best part of forty miles ahead of me, down

to the Bodotria crossing, more than thirty on to Inveresk, and it was setting in for a night of wind and rain, the kind that doesn't make for speed. Soon we were travelling half-blind into the bared teeth of the storm; and after the moon went down, the night was as black as the inside of a wolf's belly. But Phaedrus and I both knew those hills as though they were part of us, and he never slackened speed up hill or down. Aye, he was the best horse I ever had, and I came near to breaking him that night.

He was sobbing for breath as we headed down at last into the level country north of the Firth and was beginning to reel in his tracks. I fondled his neck and made much of him, shouted to him above the wind and rain, 'Hold up, boy, not long now! Warm stable soon and hot mash! Hold on, old hero!' And he flicked back his ears for the sound of my voice and plunged valiantly on.

We turned westward, keeping the faint paleness of the Bodotria Firth on our left – water shows pale, even on the darkest night – and after that it was somewhat easier going, with the wind behind us; and well before the end of the third watch, we came down to the military ferry, and saw the glimmer of firelight through the guard-hut doorway.

I slipped from Phaedrus' back, shouting before my feet were on the ground: 'Ferry! Guard ho!'

They tumbled out, sleepy and cursing. I never knew the ferry guard yet that didn't regard it as a personal affront if anyone wished to use the ferry.

But I'd no time for their grumbles. I thrust Phaedrus upon the first comer: 'Here, take my horse and see to him. Give him a hot mash, he's about done. Boatman, quickly, man! I must be in Inveresk by dawn!'

The boatman came, and the light, skin-clad corough was run down into the water. I climbed aboard, and the boatman bent to the paddle. It was a choppy crossing, and a slow one. But we made it at last, and I got a fresh horse on the further side – they kept a few there, for it was a posting station in those days – and was on my way again. Again the loneliness of night and storm and horse's hooves, but now at least there was a road to guide me, which was as well, for I was almost past finding the way for myself, if the post horse hadn't known it.

I got another remount at the Cramond fort; and with the first sullen streaks of a low dawn showing yellow over the firth, I was beating on the gates of the naval fort.

'Open, in Caesar's name!'

Inside, I heard the sounds of the Gate Guard turning out, and from overhead, the sentry's challenge: 'Who comes?'

I shouted back: 'Frontier Scout from Credigone garrison, with urgent word for the Commander.'

Inside there was a barked order. The gates swung open just wide enough to let a horse and rider through, and the Optio of the Gate Guard stood in my path.

'What word for the Commander? Not being a night owl nor yet a wolf, the Commander doesn't hold with being hauled out of bed this early without a good reason.'

'There's reason enough,' I said, dismounting. 'I've not come down from Tavaside through the night and half killed a good horse under me to tell him it's a foul morning.'

'The reason first,' he said.

So I gave it him, and watched his eyes widen in the light of the paling torches. 'Saxon war-boats, beached where they've no business to be.'

There was a moment of silence; then he said to the man nearest to him: 'Go and fetch the Duty Centurion.'

The Duty Centurion came, hitching at his sword belt, and a very short while later, I was in the Fort Commander's quarters, standing before the Fort Commander himself with his hair on end and a cloak hastily flung on over his under-tunic.

I showed him Rufus' ring, and made my report in as few words as possible. He looked at the ring closely, by the smoky light of the freshly lit oil-lamp, then nodded, and returned it.

'So, the Sea Wolves have turned to Northern waters. Two ships, you say? And an envoy with a green branch?'

'Reinforcements will be on their way from Credigone by now, Sir,' I said urgently. 'But I doubt there'll be enough to handle two full fighting crews,

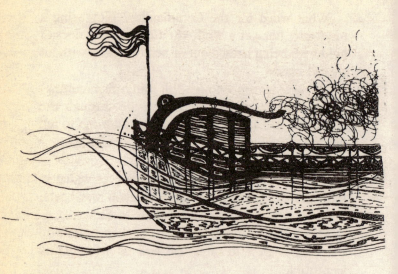

and unless the Saxons can be cut off from the sea. . . .'

'Yes, I do understand the situation.' The Commander thrust his chair back screeching on the tiled floor, and got up. 'Centurion Galba, the Thetis and Thunderer are ready for sea?'

The tall Centurion who had come in after me said, 'And Orion, Sir.'

'So, then we'll send up the three of them. Notify their Trierarchs and the Centurions of Marines – Brother Wolf, could you recognize this inlet from the seaward side?'

'Yes, Sir, I think so.'

'Good! Then you will go with the Thunderer.'

I shook off somehow the leaden weight of weariness that had begun to settle down on me,

making everything vaguely unreal, and managed a reasonable salute as I turned to follow Centurion Galba.

The next thing I knew at all clearly was the live feel of a galley's deck under my feet. And after that there was a time of orderly confusion, of men hurrying, as it seemed to me, all ways at once, and trumpet calls, and shouted orders to cast off and out oars. The navy don't waste time, I'll say that for them, and before full daylight, Thunderer, Thetis and Orion were heading down the firth, the rowers swinging to their oars in time to the clack of the Hortator's hammer. The galleys rose and dipped like gulls into the short choppy seas. I'd had no breakfast, and I wasn't sorry.

The marine next to me said, cheeringly: 'Wait

till we meet open water! Thunderer's the worst sea-boat in the Patrol Fleet – rolls like a farrowing sow!'

I groaned. It was bad enough in the firth. I didn't want to know what it would be like outside.

'Never been to sea before?'

I shook my head. 'And I hope I never go to sea again. I'm a Frontier Wolf, not a Sea Wolf. Give me a horse between my knees and I'm fine – but *this*. . . .'

He laughed. 'Och, the sea's well enough when you get used to it, and talking of Frontier Wolves – where's your wolfskin cloak?'

'Still on the wolf who grew it,' I said. 'I've not had much time for hunting, yet, nor much luck when I've had the time.'

'Ah, well!' He stood, with his thumbs in his belt, balancing himself easily on the heaving deck, a man secure and comfortable in his own world. 'Better luck with today's kind of hunting, eh?'

But I was leaning over the rail, too busy getting rid of meals I couldn't even remember eating to reply.

The wind had gone round, and all down the firth we had it behind us to help the rowers, and made good speed accordingly; but a while after noon, we were beating up round the Ness, the wind and tide setting against each other; then indeed, with our one sail reefed, I learned whether or not the Thunderer could roll! The misery of those hours seemed to stretch into an eternity of time. But at last the Ness was behind us, and the helmsman put the steering oar hard over, and we headed in towards the Firth of Tava; and then at least we were going with the seas and not across them. ('Pull-pull-pull,' sounded the Hortator's hammer, and the galley ploughed forward to the swing of the oars.) After what had gone before, the motion seemed almost gentle. I think I even slept a little, miserably huddled in my cloak in the shelter of the bulwarks.

It was dusk when we gained the mouth of the Tava, and we went in, in line-abreast, in hope of sighting the Sea Wolves between us if they should be already making for open water; though the Gods knew how slim a hope that was, in the dusk and the driving rain-squalls! Soon enough – for of course we could show no lights – we were lost to sight of each other, and I'm thinking a full war-fleet could have slipped through our guard, and us none the wiser, in those first few miles before the firth began to narrow. Then Thetis and Orion loomed out of the murk again, and took station behind us, and Och! it was good to be in quiet water once more! And the Trierarch called me to join him and the Centurion in the prow.

'You know all this coast,' he said, when I stood beside him.

'I've ridden the southern shore often enough – and looked northward across the river with my eyes open in my head.'

'So, then keep them open in your head now. How far do you judge us to be from this inlet of yours?'

'Four – five miles, maybe,' I said. 'It would be easier to be sure if the moon would break through this murk.'

'I'm not doubting it,' said the Centurion, 'do the best you can.'

For a good way we slipped on up-river, and then the northern skyline began to take on a familiar shape that had for me the right 'feel' even in that stormy darkness. I suppose I tensed, like a hunting dog that scents the quarry, for the trierarch beside me said quickly: 'Getting near?'

'I think, getting very near,' I said. But it was so hard to be sure. 'If this is the bend of the river that I think it is – if I could *see*. . . .'

The Centurion's voice sounded quick and quiet behind me. 'Men – take up fighting order.'

And I heard the faint drilled sound of feet finding an exact position, and the jink of accoutrements, as the order was carried out.

The Thunderer nosed round the bluff that thrust out there into the river, and as the next stretch opened to us, I was sure!

'Yes! Beyond the woods yonder – there, where the spur of the hillside breaks away.'

Almost in the same instant we heard the mating-call of a wolf, twice repeated, and from somewhere among the hazel woods where yesterday I had lain looking down at the Saxon galleys, a she-wolf answered.

'Ours, or theirs?' the Centurion asked at half breath.

'Ours! I know the signal.'

And then we were edging over into the mouth of the inlet that had opened suddenly in the northern shoreline. The wind and the hiss of the next rain-squall covered the dip of our oars; and there, ahead of us, against the dark fleece of hazel and alder scrub, was the glim of a shielded light, and shapes moving on the paler darkness of the water.

I let my breath go in a small sigh; and the trier-arch answered as though I had spoken. 'Aye, and making ready for sea, by the look of it. Trumpeter – sound the Attack!'

The trumpet yelped through the wind and rain, and the galley leapt forward as the rowers bent to their oars and drove her through the water. I felt her like a live thing under me, gathering herself to spring. The Trierarch's shouted order followed hard on the echo of the trumpet: 'Stand by to ram! – *Now!*'

We bore down upon the nearest of the dark shapes. There was a grinding crash, and the Thunderer shuddered from stem to stern as the bronze-sheathed ram went home. We backed water, shaking off our kill, and, in the same instant, it was as though all Tartarus broke loose.

It was an odd sort of fight, fought out part on shipboard, part in the shallows under the bank, for, after the rams had done their work, half of us went overboard to meet the Saxons in the water, while three patrols of the Frontier Wolves came yelling down through the hazel scrub to take them from

the shoreward side. The Sea Wolves fought like
heroes, I'll give them that. And soon there was light
to fight by – the red glare of burning warboats –
for, seeing the thing hopeless, they must have fired
their own keels, rather than let the rammed hulks
fall into our hands. Aye, and the flare of them might
like enough have brought the Picts down on us at
any moment! Maybe the Sea Wolves had thought
of that, too!

I was with the Marines, and I wanted to get
through to my own kind, but there was a man in
the way, a chief of some sort, swinging a great axe,
with a knot of his carles round him. I saw in the
flame-light the magnificent black wolfskin cloak
that was flung back from his shoulders, and an idea
came to me, one of those crazed ideas one gets in
time of battle. And I made for him, howling, the
Marines splashing after me and giving tongue with
their own war cry as they came. The water was no
more than knee deep, just there under the bank.
We cut our way through the bodyguard, and I
remember diving in under the shining sweep of that
tremendous war-axe. Surely I had a charmed life
that night! And my swordpoint took him under the
golden collar and grated on the bones at the back
of his neck. He went down like a poled ox, his life
gushing out red into the shallows. He was a big
man, with a broad, simple face, and wide-set eyes
that stared straight back into mine, dead though he
was, as I hauled him up to get at the gold clasp at
his shoulder. But it wasn't the clasp I wanted, and

when it came free, I dropped it into the water, and dragged clear the dripping wolfskin cloak.

Then I looked round for more fighting, but it was as good as over.

Later, while the galleys were ferrying us across the river, I heard Decurian Rufus giving his account of things to the Trierarch and the Centurion of Marines. 'They waited till nightfall, and then sent off two more men; I suppose to find out what had become of their herald. Curithir,' he jerked his chin toward the small, dark shadow squatting at his side, 'and a couple of my lads went after them, and made sure that they should not come back either. And the rest must have decided it wasn't exactly healthy on these shores, and began making ready for sea. We waited as long as we could, and we were just going to have a try at settling them without your help – '

'You'd not have stood much chance,' said the Centurion.

'No, I don't suppose we should; but we could not just have sat there on our haunches, twiddling our thumbs, and watched them out to sea. Och, well! Before we had to put it to the test, we heard the look-out's signal and knew that you were here.'

They landed us on the southern shore in the first light of a storm-spent dawn; and we were glad enough of the lift. It mightn't have been exactly healthy for us either, trying to make our way back up-river to the crossing-place through Pictish territory; not after that night's work! And we set off up

Tavaside yet again – the three patrols of us this time, minus casualties – to pick up the horses. I had the great wolfskin bundled on my shoulder. Full of water it was, and weighed a goodish deal.

Decurian Rufus looked at it aside. 'What in Mithras's name have you got there?'

'My wolfskin,' I said. 'A sea-wolfskin – off the Chief I killed.'

Curithir gave the soft quick laugh of his kind. 'I saw him. Truly, they say the Frontier Wolves are all mad.'

Aye, that was a patrol worth remembering; and for more reasons than one! It was the first time the Saxon wind blew on our northern coasts. North and South and East, it blows upon them all nowadays, while the Scots come thrusting in from Hibernia across the Western sea. But none the less, for a little while, we had flung back the new danger.

And I had gained me my wolfskin cloak.

6

The Eagles Fly South AD 383

When I was ten summers old, I found a bit of blue glass sticking out of the earth, where a badger had dug himself a new door-hole in the rough hummocky ground south of the fort. It was part of a bowl or jug, I suppose. When you looked through it, it made the whole world look blue and strange. I kept it for three days, and then exchanged it with another boy for a freshly cast viper's skin that he had found close by. You never knew what you might find in that piece of rough ground.

Old Paulus, who had served the length and breadth of the Wall and its outposts, told me that there were hummocky patches south of every fort – the remains of towns that had been there when he was a young soldier. There used to be wine shops and bath-houses and market places, he said, and the temples of many Gods, all falling into ruin since the faith of the Christos became the official religion of the Empire; and the bothies where the soldiers lived with their women and children close under the fortress walls. The towns were all wrecked and burned down in the great Pictish Wars before I was born. And when the fighting was over, they were never rebuilt. Instead, the forts were patched up, and the people who were left alive moved inside them, and the wine shops and markets and married quarters sprang up again within the walls, so that every fort became a little walled town. My fort, my town, was Onnum, where the old North Road from Corstopitum goes through into nowhere. Old Paulus used to say that any Centurion of *his* day would weep to see the place now. It is in my mind that that is a thing old soldiers have been saying since the Legions first began; but it is in my mind also that this time maybe it was true.

'Whole families *and* the family pig squatting in the granaries and the old stables,' he would grumble, wagging his head, 'half the Praetorium given over to stores, and an armoury where we used to house the Cohort Standards and the altars to the Gods.' (Paulus was one of those, there were a good many in the army, who obeyed the Imperial orders about worshipping the Christos in public, but kept the old Gods in their hearts, and to him, the Sacellum where the standards were housed was also the place for their altars.)

But we liked things well enough as they were. My father was Number Three Centurion of a Spanish Cohort, but himself was born and bred north of the Wall, like most of our family since the Eagles flew north from Rome. And my mother was pure British, from the Dumnoni who have their hunting runs over to the north-west. For a long time I was the only young-one – there were two sons born after

me but they both died – so my father and I were
very much together, working in our field plots. The
garrisons of all the forts farmed the land round
about, holding it from the Government, in part
return for military service. That was another thing
Paulus didn't like. He said a good soldier shouldn't
have time to be a farmer too. But I don't know. . . .
The Tribes were quiet in those days, and in a way,
friendly, though it was a kind of armed friendliness.
They needed us as much as we needed them,
against the threat of the Sea Wolves and the Scots.

I remember one evening, it must have been
around four years after I found the bit of blue glass,
I came up from working on our field plot. It was a
hot still day, which is a thing you don't often get
along the Wall, and at the sheltered end of the plot,
where the land tipped southward, our bean rows
were all in flower; it seemed as though life had
always been as it was that day, and would go on
being the same for ever. Paulus was sitting in the
sun by the south gate – what they used to call the
Praetorian Gate – mending a broken harness strap.
He was past bearing arms or working in the fields,
but he was good with his hands, and he hated
having nothing to do, and so he was generally
mending something for somebody.

I squatted down beside him to watch what he
did: 'That's a neat mend. What news have you
today?'

He spat out the leather thong that he had been
softening between his toothless gums. 'What makes

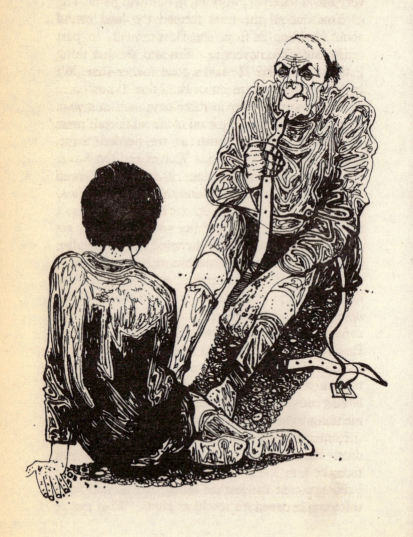

you think that I have any? An old man sitting in the sun?'

'You always gather all the news of the fort,' I said. 'Besides, it's in your face.'

He said, 'We have a new Emperor.'

'East or West?' I was not over-interested. We had split the Empire into two before I was born; and there was an Emperor in Rome and another in Constantinople, as well as two, one might call them Lieutenant Emperors, who had the title of Caesar, but were less important than the others. They were generally fighting among themselves, and it was all very complicated; in any case it seemed a long way off from the Wall.

'Neither,' he said, 'an Emperor of Britain.'

That was quite a different thing! And it made a kind of jolt in the pit of my stomach. *'Britain!* Who?'

He knotted off the thong, and cut the end almost savagely. Then he said: 'Maximus.'

I caught my breath. 'Maximus? You mean – *our* General Maximus? The one father served under in the Pict War?'

'I also, come to that.'

Suddenly, for a heart-beat of time, it seemed to me that all the colours of the evening were brighter than life; it was a moment of splendour that caught at my throat, and I wanted to shake the old man to make him feel it too. 'An Emperor of our *own*! Paulus, you're looking for all the world as though it were bad news!'

'Am I?' he grunted. 'Och, well, I've seen Emperors come and go. They do it rather often nowadays. I've seen the roads they follow, and where the roads lead them. Maximus won't be able to stop at Britain; the others will break him if he does. He'll have to try for Gaul. And if he gets Gaul – he'll try for Rome itself. And he'll take troops out of Britain. They always take troops out of Britain. And every time the end is darkness.'

He began gathering his things together, and would not say any more, except that the sun was westering and the evening air was cold for old bones.

And sure enough, before many months had passed, we heard that our Emperor Maximus was sailing for Gaul and taking British troops with him. But they were not northern troops, and so none of that touched the Wall; and the beans ripened and we harvested the oats and barley; and the winter was a hard one and brought the wolves in close to the fort. From time to time we heard of attacks by the Sea Wolves as men called the Saxons, away down the eastern coasts of Britain. And the Commander of Onnum tightened up on discipline and ordered more arms drills and a constant watch kept on the signal stations from the South. So my father was kept busy, and more of the farm work than usual fell on my shoulders, while he attended to his Centurion's duties. But truth to tell, none of it came as close to me as the fact that that summer my mother started another baby.

I was outraged! I remember standing and staring at her with startled disapproval when she told me.

'But Mother, you're *old*! *I'm* nearly fifteen!'

She looked up from the patch that she was putting into the shoulder of my father's workaday cloak. 'And, to be sure, that is a great age! I was not two years older when I started you!'

'Everybody will laugh!' I said, 'and by the time he is old enough for the army, I shall be so far ahead I shall not even be able to help him.'

'Will you be already a General? Or an Emperor, perhaps? Think what an Emperor could do for his fifteen-years-younger brother!'

'Now *you* are laughing.'

'Only because I'm happy,' she said.

And I remembered the two brothers born after me, and did not say any more.

After a time I began to think that it might not be so bad – once he got past the wet and wailing stage. I saw myself teaching him how to use a sling and how to tickle for trout in the little burn that ran below the fort. But when the baby came, just at the time that the little cold primroses were opening in the sheltered hollows, it was a girl! It was funny, I'd never thought of that. I don't think my mother had either. By my father seemed not ill-pleased.

One evening, when I'd come home from the fields to find supper not yet ready, and our quarters more than usually full of women – it's often like that in a house where there's a new baby, have you noticed? – I went up to the ramparts to while away the time until there should be something to eat. Officially, only the men on duty were supposed to go up there, but in truth, nobody took much notice, unless you got in the way of the sentries or started playing the fool with the great catapults.

On the ramparts there seemed always to be a wind, and you could look away and away – northward, over the heather country towards the land of the Picts, or southward, over more heather country, along what was left of the old military road, towards the great cities where I had never been and the fortresses of the Saxon shore. And east and west, you could follow the line of the Wall itself, looping and rising and dipping until it was lost in distance, along the high crests of the land. And as I looked eastward, I saw a little cloud of dust on the road that follows the Wall. It grew bigger, and I could make out a seed of darkness at its heart; and the seed of darkness grew to be a horse and rider travelling at full gallop.

I heard the trumpet sound, and saw the Optio of the Gate Guard, small-seeming as a games-piece at that distance, walk forward to meet the rider as he swept in through the shadowed archway and brought his horse to a trampling halt. The man dismounted heavily, as one that had ridden far as well as hard; and while somebody led his horse away, I watched him follow the Duty Centurion in the direction of the Commander's quarters, until they were both hidden from me by the clutter of buildings between. And it was as small as pieces moving on a games-board, so small, you couldn't think it really meant anything.

By dusk, the news was running through Onnum that the Emperor Maximus had landed at Segedunum to make an inspection of the Wall.

I met Paulus on my way home, and asked him the meaning of the news. 'What's bringing him back from Gaul, then? – It couldn't really be just to inspect the Wall?'

'Men,' Paulus said. 'To help him finish with the young Gratian. He'll be wanting more men; they always do.'

In our quarters, late that night, while my mother sat spinning, and crooning to the girl-child beside the fire, I helped my father burnish his weapons and equipment – not that there was much need; he always kept his tack in full-dress order.

We had been working for a good while in silence. Most likely we were both busy with the same thought. At last I came out with it. 'Paulus says that the Emperor has come back from Gaul because he needs more men.'

'Paulus is probably right,' said my father, breathing on his helmet and rubbing hard.

'Men from the Wall?' I said, after the silence had gone on for what seemed a long time.

'Maybe.'

'But the Wall garrisons are under-strength as it is.'

My father laid aside the helmet, and looked up,

holding out his hand: 'Here, give me that. By the Lord Mithras, have I never taught you how to burnish a sword blade?'

As I told you, we were all Christians when I was a boy, by order of the Emperor before the Emperor before the last one. But there were times when my father, like Paulus, turned back to old Gods with whom he was more at home. And when that happened, I knew that it was time for me to shut my mouth. So I shut it, and turned myself to polishing up the family bracelet – an old and much battered Distinguished Conduct bracelet of the Second Augustan Legion, that had belonged to some ancestor of ours, and been north of the Wall just about as long as we had. My father kept it with his own equipment, and always wore it on full-dress occasions, pushed up high under his sleeve so that it hardly showed – which was odd, when you come to think of it. . . .

Well, so Maximus came.

Officially it was called an Inspection, and it started that way – I watched from a distance, lying up on the south rampart, with most of the other boys of the fort. But, as soon as the Parade was over, it turned into something more like a riot, as his old soldiers broke ranks and came clamouring round him, shouting his name: 'Maximus! Magnus Maximus! Where are the wine skins? How can we drink good luck to you, if you don't bring us the wine? Maximus, do you remember the old war cry?

How about it, General – when do we march on Rome?'

And that was the only sight I ever had of our Emperor: a big, square-cut man wearing a cloak of the Imperial Purple, and riding a tall roan horse, with a yelling mob of soldiers surging around him who looked as though they might have him out of the saddle at any moment. But he wasn't the kind that comes out of the saddle easily; even at a distance I could see that. And it came to me suddenly, for the first time, that he was only just *one* man, and he had all our fates – ours on the Wall, and the fates of Britain and Gaul and maybe of Rome as well – tangled up with his own along with the reins in his bridle hand. And I was half-wild with excitement and half-cold afraid.

He stayed two days at Onnum, and then he moved on down the Wall. And after he was gone, my father came back to our quarters at the time of the evening meal.

He sat down and stretched his feet to the fire, for the spring chill was still in the air, though it was drawing on to summer. And he said: 'Paulus was right. Our Emperor Maximus wants men.'

My mother looked up from the little hot loaves she was piling on to a platter, and said one word, very quietly: 'You?'

'Yes,' my father said. 'Four Centuries from Onnum; the Third among them. More than half the strength!'

My mother set the platter down. She had gone

very white, and her eyes looked like dark holes in her face. 'But – *you?*'

'I am the Centurion of the Third Century,' my father said simply.

I got up and left them, and went and lay on my stomach in the hummocky ground where once I had found my piece of blue glass that made all the world look strange. I did not want any supper, though I had been hungry enough a short while ago. Presently I heard footsteps brushing through the long grass, and someone sat down beside me. I rolled over, and it was my father, his face outlined darkly against the evening sky.

I began to pull up grass stems; I remember now the little sharp snapping sounds they made. 'When do you leave?'

'The third morning from now.'

I sat up quickly. 'Let me come with you.'

'No,' he said, flatly and deliberately.

'But – ' I began. He did not seem to hear me, only his own thoughts inside his head. 'Why not?'

He heard that. 'For one thing, you are too young.'

'Among the Tribes, I'd count as a man by now.'

'But among the Romans, and *you are Roman*, you are still too young for the army by two good years.'

'In ordinary times, yes, but – '

'But these are not ordinary times, exactly.' He took me by the shoulders and looked at me very straightly; even in the fading light I could see something in his face, in his way of looking, that I had never seen before. 'Lucian, I shall have my hands full in these next three days. We may not have much chance to speak together again; so listen to me now. I need you too much to take you with me. I need you *here*! Here, to look after your mother and the small-one, and the farm-holding, until I come back.'

'If you come back,' I said, desperately.

'If Maximus fails, I think that none of us will come back. If that is the way it goes, then more than ever, I shall need you here. We have distant kinsfolk among the Votadini – bronzesmiths at Traprain Law; you have heard me speak of them. If I do not come back, take your mother and the small sister to them. I leave them in your keeping.'

We looked at each other long and long. And in the end I accepted the way that I knew the thing had to be. 'Yes, Father.'

As he said, we had little chance to speak together after that, and I did not ask him again to let me go with the troops, though some of the other boys, little older than I, were going. I had learned long before, that if my father did not say: 'Yes', at the first asking, he would not change because one asked again – or twenty times again!

So the third morning came, and the four Centuries of the Cohort marched out, my father's Century leading them; out through what used to be the Praetorian Gate, and away down the road that led to Corstopitum – and Gaul – and Rome. I heard the trumpets sounding back on the wind, and a child cried somewhere in the watching crowd, and a dog barked, in the sudden emptiness that they left behind.

It had been a dry spring, and the dust of the roadway rose in a cloud behind their marching feet, and they were lost in it.

Life went on! A couple of Centuries of Scythian Archers were moved into Onnum from Borcovicus to fill the gap a little. All along the Wall that was happening, as the remaining garrisons were spread more evenly. And I and the other boys on the edge of manhood began to take our places with the troops at weapon practice, as well as tending our fathers' field plots. And every morning we thought: 'Perhaps there will be news today.' And every night we went to sleep thinking: 'Like enough, there will be news tomorrow.'

And so spring and summer went by.

The first news reached us with the autumn gales, and went roaring from fort to fort along the Wall like a great triumphant gale itself.

'Victory! It's Victory!' everyone was telling everyone else. 'Gratian's down and dead! Maximus has dealt with the Emperor Pup! He's got all Gaul in his knapsack, and now for Rome!'

But old Paulus said, 'Aye, and now for the Emperor Theodosius!' and there was no triumph in his tone.

Two and a half years after my father went away,

the second news reached us. And that was news of a battle, too. A great battle between Maximus and Theodosius; and Maximus defeated and executed, and many of his officers with him; and the rest of his army slain or captive or scattered in flight.

We had been afraid of that news for a long time; but when it came, it was too big and terrible for us to find room in our hearts for it all at once. At first I would not believe that my father was dead, and neither would my mother. At least, I think we knew in our inmost places, but we would not admit it to each other, or to ourselves. I think there were many like us, in those first days after the word came.

'We must wait,' my mother said. 'He may have escaped. He may be on his way home even now. We will not grieve yet – not just yet.'

That was on the edge of winter. An evil winter, spent in waiting for more news that did not come; in waiting for attacks upon the Wall that did not come either. We heard of fighting on the Saxon shore; but, save for a few brushes with raiding Scots at the western end, the Wall was left to itself. It seemed that we had been forgotten, by friends and enemies alike.

'Now that the danger threatens as sharply from the South as from the North, I am thinking that the Wall has served its day,' Paulus said. 'Oh, it will last my time – I am old. Old and tired; and I too have served my day. But soon, I think that the Eagles will fly south, and all this will be forsaken, except by its dead.'

And then, at winter's end, it seemed that we were remembered again. And the Emperor Theodosius sent officers to see what should be done about the old defences that had lost their use.

They lodged a night at Onnum. And that evening a man came to the door of our quarters and beckoned me outside. I recognized him – for I had seen them ride in – as the Centurion of the Officers' Escort.

'You are Lucianus, son of Centurion Lucius Calpurnius?' he said, when I joined him in the tumbledown colonnade.

'I am,' I said, 'if that's anything to you.' I was on my guard.

He held out something that glinted faintly in the light from the open doorway. 'I have this for you. It seemed best, maybe, not to give it to you in front of your mother.'

I took the thing from him. The feel of it was so familiar in my hand that, for the moment, it seemed as though it must bring my father with it, they were so closely part of each other. 'Our bracelet! Our silver Capricorn! My father gave you this?'

He nodded: 'He asked me, if ever I could do so, to find means to get it to you. As things have turned out, it has been easy enough.'

I stood turning the bracelet over and over in my hands, trying to straighten out something that was snarled and tangled in my mind – or in my heart. 'You and my father – you were friends?'

He said in a quiet, carefully levelled voice: 'In

our young days we served together under Maximus against the Picts. Last autumn I commanded his guard on the night before his execution.'

I said, just as carefully, 'My father was – executed?'

'With others of Maximus' officers. It was cleanly done; honourably, with a sword. The same death as Maximus died; a better one than he meted out to Gratian.'

I was still turning and turning the bracelet. The feel of it seemed to help. 'It – seems my father died in good company,' I said at last.

'In the very best.'

'Was there any message with the bracelet?'

'No. He just asked me to give it to you,' the man said, and added, very kindly, 'I think the bracelet *is* the message.'

I said, 'I – I am sorry that I cannot ask you into the house.'

'I am sorry, too,' he said. 'I would have liked to come to know Lucius' son. But you cannot ask me into the house.'

So he turned away. I waited a little, outside in the dark; then I went in, and showed the bracelet to my mother. And we both knew that it was time to stop pretending.

We sat very late over the fire that night, my mother staring into the flames, and the red hollows under the flames, while I polished and re-polished the old Capricorn bracelet, and the small sister slept in the corner. My mother had not taken her into the inner room as usual. I think it was in her heart to keep us all together. I heard the trumpet sounding for the third watch of the night: the longest and the darkest watch, when people die or are born. The sound roused my mother, and she sat up and looked about her, like someone rousing from sleep, but she had not been asleep.

'There is nothing to keep us here any more,' she said.

I shook my head. 'Nothing. We will start tomorrow for Traprain Law.'

'Traprain Law?' She sounded as though she had never heard the name before that moment.

'Father said that if he did not come back, we were to go to his kinsfolk at Traprain Law.'

She sat and looked at me, unmoving and unspeaking, so long that I wondered if she did not understand. But she was perfectly calm, though dried out with grief, like the dried papery husk of a flower that has finished blooming and shaken out its goodness on the wind. 'Not Traprain Law,' she said at last, with a great pride that I had never seen in her before. 'I am not of the Votadini. I will not go among strangers, to be taken in out of pity and befriended for my dead man's sake. I am a chief's daughter. I will go back where I have the right to go – to my own people – to my father's hall.'

It seemed to me that my father would not mind. So next morning we made two bundles of the things that would come in useful: an old worn cloak of my father's amongst them. And my mother took

one, and I took the other and the small sister on my shoulder, and we set out north-westward for the hunting runs of the Dumnoni.

If my father had been killed in battle, I might have gone back when I had made sure that all was well with my mother and the small-one. There was still an army, though they had taken the garrisons from the Wall. But as it was – the time went by and the time went by; and then I married with a girl of the Tribe. And the Tribe has had need of all its fighting men, with every west wind bringing the Scots raiders, in these past years.

Soon, my sons or my sons' sons will forget that we were ever anything but tribesmen of the Dumnoni. . . . No, not quite; the Capricorn bracelet will see to that, the old battered Legionary bracelet that is our link with Rome. . . .

A few autumns ago, I went down as far as the Wall, on the hunting trail. There's good hunting that way – the wolves lair-up in the forsaken forts. No men, now, just the wolves. I haven't been back again.

Background For These Stories

AD 43   The Emperor Claudius successfully invaded Britain, and then returned to Rome to take his Triumph. The troops he left behind him to complete the conquest and become an Army of Occupation were divided into three forces, and pushed on from the south-east to make their headquarters at last in three great Legionary Stations, at Caerleon-upon-Usk (Isca Silurum), Chester (Deva) and Lincoln (Lindum). The Ninth Legion, which was stationed at Lincoln, later pushed on north again to York (Eburacum). But that was only the first stage; and in

AD 61   Suetonius Paulinus, the Governor General, took a large force into North Wales to deal with troubles among the tribes there. He was in Anglesey, campaigning against the Druids, who were the heart and core of the 'Resistance Movement' when Queen Boudicca of the Iceni started her uprising in the East of Britain.

AD 80–85   Gnaeus Julius Agricola fought his great Northern Campaigns, setting up legionary stations at Corbridge (Corstopitum) and Newstead (Trimontium) and then a line of forts across the Narrows from the Clyde to the Forth, and other isolated forts at the mouths of the Highland Glens. In the sixth summer he gained a crushing victory over the Northern tribes at Mons Graupius, somewhere north of where Perth stands now. But soon after, with his work still half finished, he was recalled to Rome.

AD 100–117   The Emperor Trajan fought his Dacian Campaigns. These were brilliant and successful, but desperately costly in men; and the occupying forces of the Empire were reduced to a dangerously low level to provide more. His second war in the Near East was a disaster, and news of his death was the signal for a rising among the North British tribes, in which the Ninth Legion was wiped out.

AD 117   The Emperor Hadrian came to Britain with the Sixth Legion to replace the Ninth, and determined on the building of a great frontier defence across North Britain. This was probably begun in AD 23

AD 122   and finished about five years later.

AD 142   Lollius Urbicus built the Antonine Wall, largely on the line of Agricola's old Clyde-Forth string of forts. He also rebuilt the big Outpost Stations such as Newstead, and turned the country between the Walls – roughly speaking, Lowland Scotland – into a sort of buffer territory to take the main shock of troubles in the North from Hadrian's Wall.

AD 155   The Northern tribes again revolted, the whole North dissolved in chaos, and by

AD 162   the Antonine Wall was lost, Newstead and the rest of the outpost forts destroyed. A temporary Roman victory followed, and again the forts were restored, but in

AD 184   there was a still more violent revolt, and despite another Roman victory, there was never again a full-scale Roman military occupation north of Hadrian's Wall. Instead, a new kind of government began; and the Lowlands became a kind of Protectorate. Tribal boundaries were formally defined, and the amount of tribute to be paid in cattle, grain and young men for the Army all agreed; tribal gatherings for trade and other purposes were limited to fixed times and places under Roman supervision

AD 196   Clodius Albinus, Governor of Britain, took most of the British-based troops to the Continent in an attempt to wrest the Imperial Throne from Septimus Severus. On his defeat at Lyons, the Northern tribes revolted yet again, the Wall went up in flames and devastation spread as far south as York. Severus sent reinforcements under a new Governor, Varus Lupus, who dealt with the uprising and divided the country into two provinces, Upper and Lower Britain.

Gradually, friendship of a kind returned between Rome and the tribes, and instead of the old forced levy of young men for the Army, there began to be free local recruiting for the Auxiliaries.

AD 209　But the North could not be counted as secure, until the Highland tribes from beyond the old Northern Wall, the Picts, the Caledonii had been taught a lesson they would not forget. The Emperor Severus himself led two punitive expeditions against them, but on

AD 211　the eve of the third, he died at York. His half-mad son, Caracalla, who took over from him, did not push the third campaign through. So the Highland tribes were saved, but nevertheless, they had learned their lesson, and the Lowlands had nearly a hundred years of comparative peace. Again the old outpost forts were rebuilt, and now some of them began to serve as bases for long-range scouts, who patrolled well north of the Tweed and probably as far north as the Tay. Friendly relations between Rome and the Lowland tribes continued, probably because of the growing menace of the Scots from Ireland, the Caledonii, when they began to forget their lesson, and the distant tidings of Saxon raiders in the South.

AD 284　Diocletian became Emperor, and, while himself keeping the supreme command, divided the rule of the Empire into four, and took a fellow Emperor and two 'Lieutenants' who bore the title of Caesar. In

AD 313   he died, and after ten years' Civil War, Constantine the Great became Emperor.

AD 334   Constantine proclaimed Christianity the official religion of the Roman State, and at the same time divided the Empire into East and West by making a new capital at Byzantium, which he renamed Constantinople.

AD 337   Constantine died, and for the next five years the rival Caesars struggled for power, while the frontiers of the Empire began to crumble.

AD 342   There was another crisis of some sort in Britain, of which no one quite knows the details, and as usual the forts were destroyed. Constans, the Emperor of the moment, came and restored the situation; and also saw to the building of Anderida (Pevensey in Sussex), the last of the long chain of Saxon shore forts to be built, in an attempt to hold off the sea raiders.

AD 364   Two Emperors later, Valens was appointed to rule the West by Valentinian, Emperor of the East, and for a time managed to hold off the barbarians who were attacking his half of the Empire on all sides.

AD 368   Meanwhile, Scots, Caledonii, Jutes and Saxons were breaking in on Britain from every quarter. The Roman General in the North was ambushed and killed at the same time as the Count of the Saxon Shore was defeated by sea raiders. Valentinian, who happened to be in France, quickly sent his best general, Theodosius, with reinforcements, to save the situation, and in the fighting which followed, 'The Pict War'.

AD 369 Theodosius cleared the coasts and rounded up the Saxon warbands that were terrorizing the countryside, then turned upon the Pictish invaders who had come swarming over the Wall to carry their own kind of fire and sword almost the length of the land, and dealt with them very thoroughly. And finally, with what he could scrape together from the remains of the British Fleet, he drove the Scots back to their own shores. Then he returned to the Continent, where a few years later he was disgraced and executed.

AD 383 Magnus Maximus, a Spanish General who had served under Theodosius in the Pict War, and held high command in Britain, was proclaimed Emperor by his troops. He crossed to France, taking some of the Legions and a large force of Auxiliaries with him, and defeated Gratian, the Emperor of the West, who was soon afterwards murdered at Lyons.

After the events described in the last story:

AD 388 Maximus himself was defeated and executed by another Emperor, Theodosius, son to his old commander of the Pict Wars. In spite of old accounts of a final great attack, it seems likely that the Wall, which no longer served much purpose now that attacks were as likely to come from the South as from the North, was simply abandoned at this time. The Imperial Frontiers were crumbling everywhere.

AD 410 The Goths sacked Rome itself, and this is generally taken as being the year in which the last Roman troops were withdrawn from Britain altogether.

But nobody is quite sure about that any more. In fact the more the experts find out about the last years of Roman Britain, the less they can be sure of anything. For the beginning of Rome-in-Britain is clear-cut and simple, but the end is chaos.

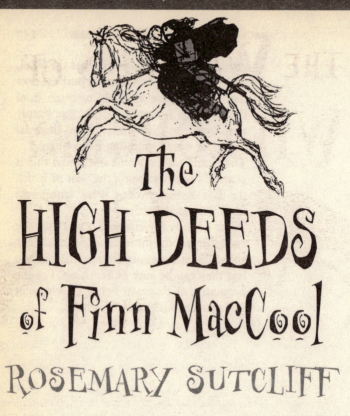

The
HIGH DEEDS
of Finn MacCool

ROSEMARY SUTCLIFF

Then the giant sprang up and seized his club and aimed three mighty blows at Dearmid, which he only just managed to turn on his upflung shield. But he knew that Sharvan expected him to attack with his sword, and so he flung it aside, and the shield with it, and leaping in beneath the giant's guard, twisted his arms about the huge body, and heaving with all his might, flung him over his shoulder and crashing to the ground.

Set in the times of enchanted beasts, fairies and strange creatures, discover the traditional irish legends of Finn MacCool and the Fianna.

ISBN 0099414228 £4.99

THE WOLVES OF WILLOUGHBY CHASE

JOAN AIKEN

*She woke suddenly to find that the train had stopped with a jerk.
'Oh! What is it? Where are we?' she exclaimed before she could stop herself.
'No need to alarm yourself, miss,' said her companion. 'Wolves on the line,
most likely – they often have trouble of that kind hereabouts.'
'Wolves!' Sylvia stared at him in terror.*

After braving a treacherous journey through snow-covered wastes
populated by packs of wild and hungry wolves, Sylvia joins her cousin
Bonnie in the warmth and safety of Willoughby Chase. But with
Bonnie's parents overseas and the evil Miss Slighcarp left in charge, the
cousins soon find their human predators even harder to escape.

'Joan Aiken is such a spellbinder that it all rings true...'
THE STANDARD

ISBN 0099411865 £4.99

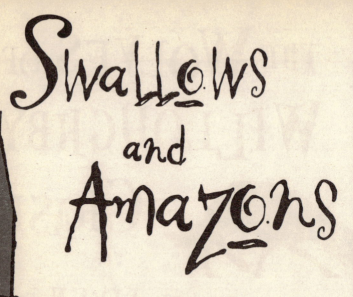

Swallows
and
Amazons

Arthur Ransome

Titty drew a long breath that nearly choked her.
'It is…' she said.
The flag blowing in the wind at the masthead of the little boat was
black and on it in white were a skull and two crossed bones.
The four on the island stared at each other.

To John, Susan, Titty and Roger, being allowed to use the boat *Swallow* to go camping on the island is adventure enough. But they soon find themselves under attack from the fierce Amazon Pirates, Nancy and Peggy. And so begins a summer of battles, alliances, exploration and discovery.

By the winning author of the first Carnegie medal.

ISBN 0099503913 £4.99